Amy Redek

Summer
AT THE VILLA

GAY EROTICA

Please feel free to send me an email. Just know that these emails are filtered by my publisher. Good news is always welcome.

Amy Redek - **amy_redek@awesomeauthors.org**

You might also want to check my blog for Updates and interesting info. http://amy-redek.awesomeauthors.org/

About the Publisher

4Fun Publishing, a member of **BLVNP Incorporated**, 340 S. Lemon #6200, Walnut CA 91789, info@blvnp.com / legal@blvnp.com
NOTE: Due to the highly emotional reaction of some people to works of erotic fiction, any email sent to the above address that contains foul language or religious references is automatically deleted by our anti-spam software and will not be seen. All other communications are welcome.

DISCLAIMER

Please don't be stupid and kill yourself. This book is a work of FICTION. Do not try any new sexual practice that you find in this book. It is fiction and not to be confused with reality. Neither the author nor the publisher or its associates assume any responsibility for any loss, injury, death or legal consequences resulting from acting on the contents in this book. Every character in this book is over 18 years of age. The author's opinions are not to be construed as the opinions of the publisher. The material in this book is for entertainment purposes ONLY. Enjoy.

Summer at the Villa

Gay Erotica

By: Amy Redek

© Amy Redek 2014
ISBN: 978-1-62761-690-4

CHAPTER I

I remember the day quite clearly for it was a Friday, the day we broke up from college for the summer holidays. I'd just got home and found mum all bubbly with excitement. There was only her there for she and dad had got divorced some four years ago and so there was only the two of us.

'Toby!' she cried. Well that was my name and it was rather apt when you considered that my surname was Jugg. 'Toby. You know those designs that I sent off to New York?' to which I nodded. 'Well they want me to go over there with my samples to display.' Mum was a dress designer and did most of her work at home, the drawings that is, while the actual shop, if you can call it that, was not far from home where the designs were turned into dresses. It wasn't exactly a sweatshop, but not far off and this was the break she had been looking forward to.

'But….oh shit! I can't take you with me. Sorry,' she said, tears in her eyes. 'But I've had an idea! How would you like to spend the summer with your grandad in Spain?'

'Er…that's great mum, you getting that chance you've dreamed of, but, er, well, would he have me. He's never seen me before,' I said.

'Nonsense! Of course he knows you,' she said. 'He's had pictures from me ever since you were baby when your father and I adopted you. Would you like to go? It's a big house and it's got a swimming pool in the garden. You'd like that wouldn't you?'

'Yes, but….' I didn't get a chance to say anymore.

'That's settled then,' and off she disappeared into what she called her office. A spare room we had that she used, for that's where she had her drawing board as well as all the tools of her trade plus her computer. I slowly followed her in there to see that she was onto an airlines page already. Her fingers flew across the keys, putting in my name, passport number and the rest and putting in her credit card number to pay for the ticket and finally inserting paper into the printer, she printed out my boarding paper.

'This is all you need,' she said waving the two papers at me. 'One for departure and the other for coming back. Oh, you'll have to show your passport too.' I had butterflies in my stomach for even though I'd had a passport for two years, this would be the first time that it was going to be used. And flying in a plane! Another first.

'But…but you haven't even spoken to grandad yet,' I said, somewhat alarmed. 'What if he's not there? What if he says no?'

'Knowing your grandfather, he'll say yes,' she said with a smile. 'He's been on his own now for the last three years and I'm absolutely sure he will say yes. Don't forget, he's only seen photos of you over the years and no doubt would like to see you in the flesh.' How right she was with this last remark.

So back into the lounge we went and she sat down by the phone and dialled his number and it only took a few minutes before she was speaking to him. I sat there with my fingers crossed as she spoke .

'Hello, Dad, how's things?' she asked, not hearing what he said. 'Couldn't be better. It's getting that good that I've been asked to show some of my things over in New York,' she gushed, then nodding her head at what he was saying to her. 'Ah. Now that's the rub and why I am ringing you now. It's about Toby, your adopted grandson. His father is out of the country on tour and I don't know what to do.' It was then that she in a deep breath. 'You see,' she began again. 'I've got to go over to the States next week and the summer holiday for Toby starts at the same time that I've supposed to leave and I can't take him with me. So daddy, I thought that with you being all alone out there in Spain would like some company for a while. So I wondered if he could come out to stay with you for the next six weeks until his new term begins. That's when I should be back in England. Please dad! You're the only one I can trust to look after him and not let him get up to any mischief.'

I couldn't hear what his reply to that little bombshell was, though he told me later.

'He would daddy. I've already told him of the villa you live in and that it has a lovely swimming pool and he became quite excited at the prospect of meeting you as well as having all that sun, swimming pool and all,' she pleaded. 'Please say you'll have him. It will give me peace of mind while I'm away. Please daddy, say yes.' I couldn't hear his answer but her face was lighting up. 'You're not an old fogie dad and he's sitting next to me hoping that you'll say yes. Look, oh, you can't see him but he's holding his hand up with his fingers crossed,' and began nodding her head. 'Oh thanks dad,' she said, 'that's lifted a great weight off my mind and he's even clapping his hands. I'll put him on the plane tomorrow.'

'Tomorrow?' I heard the squawk from the phone and only then looked at my boarding pass and saw that it was indeed dated for the next day. Tomorrow! The butterflies started up again and didn't catch anymore until she said the last words, 'Thanks again dad. I love you.' She nodded her head before putting the phone down and looked at me with a big smile on her face. 'All fixed with him only saying that you've got to behave yourself.'

'That I will mum, as long as he's not a tyrant,' I said.

'Tyrant? Never! He's got a heart of gold and I love him for it. You will too when you've been with him for a while,' she said, not knowing how close to the truth she was that I would love him, but much further than she would have dreamed as it turned out. 'Right! Let's get you packed for we'll have to leave about eight in the morning to be at Gatwick on time.'

So for an hour I put things on the bed to be packed in my suitcase with mum putting half of the things back and picking out others but finally got round to having enough inside before locking it and taking it back downstairs. Over dinner, she told me all about the place mentioning the swimming pool at least six times which I would enjoy. She was right with this for I did like my swimming and was quite good when I did my swimming in the pool at the college.

'His bedroom is behind the lounge and there is another bedroom on the ground floor too though it only has a single bed in there, so you'll probably have the double bed upstairs. It's got its own bathroom and leads out onto the sun deck. He did say that he had a dog but I've forgotten what he called it.' She rattled on for the whole meal about the urbanisation where the house was and how far it was to the shops, things like that and carried on until it was time for bed.

I really trembled in bed that night, wondering what he was really like, for he was now sixty nine years old and I hoped that he wasn't grumpy and would like me. It was one of the few nights that I didn't masturbate before falling asleep.

=oOo=

It was my subconscious mind that woke me up at daybreak around half five in the morning and I was now getting excited in the fact that I was going to go and fly in a plane. I quickly did my bathroom things before getting dressed, these having already been laid out for me by mum the night before, and had made the coffee before she came down to the kitchen.

'My, you are eager Toby,' she said before giving me a kiss on the cheek. 'Thanks for the coffee,' as she took the mug from my hand.

'Well I am getting rather excited at having my first trip in an aeroplane and seeing grandad,' I gushed.

'Well just behave yourself,' she laughed, 'and on the plane too.' She then cooked quite a big breakfast, me saying that it was too much which she countered that the food served on this flight would be crap, she was not above swearing. 'So eat up for it'll be dinner for your next meal at grandad's.'

With breakfast over and the things washed up, we waited for the cab that she had ordered the night before to arrive to take us to the airport. This duly turned up and with us and my suitcase in the cab, an hour and a half later, were at the airport. She told the driver to wait to take her back and I towed my suitcase, it was one of those with wheels at one end, into the terminal to join the queue to have it weighed. This only took twenty minutes before I then got a big kiss and a hug from mum with her saying that I was to behave myself and that she should be back in plenty of time from New York to meet me on my return. With that, I went through passport control and gave her a last goodbye wave and followed other people to find the lounge for the passengers for my plane.

What a boring hour having to wait and have nothing to read and wished that I had one of grandad's books with me. Now that would be good reading for mum had told me not to read them as they were somewhat on the pornographic side. That kind of statement was like waving a red rag in front of a bull for I now wished that I had one there with me now and couldn't wait to read one of them. Books like that were banned at home and I had only read bits like that from one of the other boy's copy of letters in a sex magazine.

We finally boarded the plane and it was a terrific experience of feeling the surge of power as the aircraft began its run down the long runway and feeling the pressure of being pushed back into your seat and more so when it started to soar up into the air, the ground, which I could see from my window seat, rapidly falling away until we passed through wisps of cloud and out into the brightest blue sky I had ever seen. Just miles and miles of white clouds that looked like rumpled white bed sheets that were reflecting the strong sunlight. I was glued to the window for most of the journey that lasted for just under two and half hours until we were told to belt up. Not to stop speaking but fix our seat belts as we were not far off landing. This was just as thrilling to see the ground coming up the lower we got, crossing roads and seeing the small cars moving like snails and then over the perimeter fence and suddenly bumping down onto the runway and having the sudden roar of the engine being put into reverse to slow us down. I was now hooked on flying such was the thrill I got from this first flight.

The plane taxied to where we were let out of this flying tube and down a short corridor into a large area that had a moving conveyor belt that went round in a half circle and eventually started having suitcases and the like on it. I eventually saw mine come round and pulled it off the belt and started following others out of this collection area where quite a lot of people were waiting for their friends or family to show themselves.

I spotted grandad straight away having studied the latest picture of him that mum had back home, though he now had a lovely suntanned face. As I got closer to him, he having known it was me at the same time, came forward with his arms open and I dropped my case at our feet and went into his arms and got a big hug.

'Welcome to Spain Toby,' he said before letting me go to pick up the strap of my suitcase.

'Thank you, grandad. Thank you for letting me come. It's so exciting with it being my first time in a plane and the first time of being in a foreign country,' I said, or words along that line for I was still on a high from the flight. He took my arm and led me out of the terminal and into the sunlight. The heat of it struck me and made me gasp out at how hot it was. He chuckled, which had a nice sound to it, and told me that August was the hottest time out there and it wasn't long before we were in his car with my case in the boot and had the car's air-conditioning on full blast.

We were soon away from the airport and he told me of how dangerous the sun was and to be careful for it would be so easy to get sunstroke. He asked about the flight and how was Julie, that's mum's name and I told him and thanked him again for having me stay with him for the summer holidays and we talked nineteen to the dozen on the drive to his home. It felt strange to be on the wrong side of the road in the driving of the car which made him laugh when I remarked on it, wincing when he went, to my mind, round the wrong way of a roundabout.

It took a little to get used to this and not wince every time a car came towards us going in the opposite direction. I was then to look out and see the many trees that were not fenced in, being told what fruit they had, most of them being nuts. Not the trees themselves stupid, that being what was growing on them. The lemon and orange trees were easy to identify though most of these were fenced in. I remarked on the lack of greenery alongside the roads.

'Well we've had quite a hot summer. It's in the spring when we get really green on the hills and fields,' he said. We finally got onto a motorway for a short distance before turning off into what looked like a small town and was told that this was the urbanisation that he lived in. We passed a block of shops and bars and yet it still took us another fifteen minutes of passing houses after crossing a bridge and past a golf course and we pulled up outside a lovely looking villa.

'Home Toby,' he said.

'It looks great grandad,' I said clapping my hands looking at the yellow painted outside walls of the house with white balustrades up on the top part. He took my suitcase out of the car and took it into the garden, a small slope down to the steps to a patio door which he unlocked before we went in and for him to then unlock a big grill to be able to open the inner door. There was a dog barking away as the grill was unlocked and with the other door open, out bounded a black and white dog that ran circles round us as he barked and kept his tail wagging all the time as he also jumped up to lick my hand as well as that of grandad.

'What a lovely dog,' I said as I knelt down to stroke him, getting licks on my face as I did so.

'This is Tom,' he said, moving into the house where I followed him and we went up some stairs to a large bedroom with a big double bed which was the only thing up there apart from a chest of drawers and it having its own bathroom. It was also the only way to get out onto a sun terrace which I could see through the sliding glass doors. He threw my suitcase on the bed and went out onto this sun deck where there was a lounger.

'You can even sun bathe naked up here Toby,' he said with that lovely chuckle he had. 'For you can't be overlooked here,' which was true as I looked round and saw that we were higher than any other house close by.

'I like this bed grandad,' I said, bouncing on it after we went back inside.

'Well settle yourself in while I prepare dinner,' and he shooed Tom out who had followed us upstairs. It didn't take long to empty the suitcase and put my things away in the chest of drawers that was there in the room before going downstairs myself.

'Can I do anything to help grandad?' I asked on entering the kitchen.

'No thanks. Take a walk round the garden,' he said nodding in the direction of the open kitchen door. I went over and I could see that lovely swimming pool mum had told me about.

'Wow! Can I go for a swim now grandad?' I asked, quite excited at the thought.

'Of course you can,' he said with a laugh. 'It's there to be used, but only for about ten minutes for dinner should be ready by then.'

'Thanks grandad,' I said, racing upstairs to get my suit on and grabbing a towel from the bathroom, raced back down and out to the steps that went down to the patio. I threw my towel onto one of the two loungers there under the shady umbrella and not really knowing the pool yet, jumped in instead of diving. It was lovely and cool as I went under and coming up to the surface worked out which was the shallow end and which was the deep end.

I ploughed my way back and forth in that lovely cool water for a good fifteen minutes before getting out and going back upstairs as I dried myself. I say up, because with the house being on the slope that it had been built on, the kitchen was a good fifteen foot higher that the pool's patio.

'I could smell the cooking grandad,' I said as I carried on drying myself.

'Well go and get dressed for I'm dishing up in fifteen minutes,' he said. So after putting on just a pair of shorts, I went back down and had a lovely meal. Well, being on his own for so long, he was used to cooking for himself. I helped with the washing up and we sat in front of the t.v., but what was on was rubbish, so I said I wanted to go to bed. He said okay for he was all in agreement to this.

'Er, grandad,' I began, not sure what his answer was going to be for my question. 'Er, mum told me that you've written quite a few books. Can I read one of them please.' He gave out another of his chuckles and had a twinkle in his eye.

'I don't see why not. You're old enough now, come,' and so I followed him into another room on this ground floor. 'This used to be a bedroom, but I've turned it into my office and library. It had two desks with a computer on each and three, well, two and a half of the walls were just bookcases, full of? You've guessed it, books! There was also a wall mounted television as well as a video and DVD recorder. What had once been a small wardrobe, he'd put up four shelves that was full of folders and it was to these he pointed.

'There they are. Take your pick.' He said with a smile on his face. I didn't bother with checking out the titles because they wouldn't have meant a thing at the time and so pulled out the first one to hand.

'Thanks grandad,' I said, and gave him a quick kiss on the cheek. 'Goodnight then,' and left him and went upstairs to bed. Now I hadn't worn pyjamas for years now, so I was quickly undressed and in bed and began to read one of his books. I was only into page four before I had to get out of bed and go and get some toilet paper to catch my sperm for I had become aroused in just those few pages. So back into bed where I then had the book open and as I read more of the sex that he had written, I jerked myself off, coming into the toilet paper.

I don't know what time I turned the light out for I read as much as I could before doing so having jerked off another two times as the story had kept me in an almost constant erection. I must have dreamed of that story so far for in the morning I had another erection and had to jerk off again.

CHAPTER II

After getting up and having a shower, went down for breakfast and grandad asked me what I had thought of the book so far. I'm sure I blushed and it made him give out a laugh. 'I bet you jerked off last night.'

'Er… yes. It's the best I've read about two people making love,' I stammered as I tried to eat my scrambled eggs.

'How many times? Once, twice, three times?' he asked, a smile on his face.

'Er…twice,' I lied with a mumble, looking down at my plate.

'I do sometimes even though I know what the whole story is, though not as often as I used to. I'm getting a bit old now and there's not a lot of steam left in the boiler nowadays,' he said.

'You're not old grandad!' I said, now lifting my head up to look at him. 'I've seen people younger than you that look much older.'

'Thank you Toby,' he said, 'but I'm now beginning to feel my age.'

'Will you come swimming with me?' I asked.

'After the washing up,' he said, and so after we had eaten, I helped him in this and then went upstairs to put my swim suit on and found when I was back downstairs that he had a big towel round his waist, and so we went down to the pool.

'You don't really have to wear a swim suit,' he said when we were down there by the two loungers. 'The two houses either side of us are unoccupied at the moment. The people who own them only use them for their holiday breaks. The one at the bottom there,' pointing to one on the other side of the lower wall, 'is occupied, but she'll be at work now, besides, they all know that I swim in the raw.'

At this, he took his towel off and threw it onto one of the loungers and dived into the deep end of the pool. He surfaced at the shallow end and stood up and gave his head a shake, the water flying out of his hair.

'Are you sure it's alright grandad?' I asked, not ever having swum naked before.

'Of course,' he said. 'I don't mind seeing a young naked body and you've just seen mine and there's nobody to see either of us.'

I'd only briefly seen what he had in between his legs and his cock in its flaccid state was nearly as big as mine when it was erect and thought, what the hell. If he can swim naked, so could I, and quickly pulled my suit off and dived into the deep end. On reaching the end, I turned and began to really plough my way up and down the length of the pool. What a thrill I had run through my body at feeling the water swiftly run along my cock and move my balls as I swam up and down, really loving the feeling of freedom in swimming naked.

I finally came to a stop at the shallow end where he was still standing, the water level only reaching up to his navel. 'That was great grandad! I didn't know it would feel as good as that without a suit one. Why aren't you swimming?' I asked, whipping my hair back with my hands.

'I...I can't swim properly. Doggie paddle and backstroke, that's all,' he said and I could feel the shame in his voice as he admitted to this and my heart went out to him at confessing this.

'But you were in the navy?' I cried.

'There's many a sailor who cannot swim. Besides, in the sea are some rather nasty creatures and having seen some them being fished out of the ocean, put me off from learning,' he said. 'So I never really got round to being able to swim properly. It's only in this pool that I learned how to do the back stroke. This end of the pool is deep enough for me.'

He then went and did two lengths of the pool doing his backstroke that showed that he'd never learned properly at how to do that. Now I'd seen boys at school naked in the showers but never a fully grown man and couldn't really help but see his cock move about as he back stroked past me, noting that he wasn't really small in that department. He was really panting after those two lengths and went and climbed out of the pool where I was then able to see that his balls looked twice the size of mine before he picked up his towel to dry himself before lying down on a lounger that was under the shade of the umbrella. I also noticed that he was quite brown all over from his sunbathing and not have any white skin showing. Just looking down at my own body skin really showed the difference and so I was determined to get as brown as he was.

I swam up and down the pool for a while longer before getting out and drying myself before getting onto the other lounger that was out in the sun. I had laid down on my front and felt the sun really warming up my back but turned onto my side to face grandad when he spoke to me.

'Did you like the story you read last night?' he asked, and I saw his flaccid cock give a twitch as he asked this.

'I haven't read it all yet, but yes, so far it's very good,' I replied.

'Was it about male and female or male and male sex?' he asked.

'Of…of two men,' I stuttered, feeling my face go a little red and also feel my own cock give a twitch at the thought of that book.

'What was it that made you jerk off twice.'

'When…when they sucked on each other,' I managed to get out, feeling my cock now starting to rise up remembering what he had written.

'I can see that just the thought has turned you on,' he said, looking at my cock that was up and hard, sticking out from my groin. I also noticed that his had grown a bit more. 'It turns me on too like it did then and when I write about the act between two men. Though what I write is only from one side of the coin as though I've had some men suck on me, I've never sucked on another man's erection. I've often wondered what it would be like. Have you ever played with another boy's cock and sucked on it?' Now that was a real question.

'Er…well…er, I have given another boy a wank and had him do it to me but we never sucked each other,' I said, not looking at him as I said this, my face feeling quite red and hot and it wasn't from the sun.

'But you jerked off reading about it? Were you wondering, like I do sometimes, as to what it would be like having your cock sucked?'

'Y…yes,' I admitted, still not being able to look him in the eye.

'Well, as I've said, I've never sucked on one though I wouldn't mind giving it a try. You've got a nice looking cock. Would you like me to do it to you and find out if I've missed out on not doing so?' There was what I have read at being called a pregnant pause before he spoke again. 'I wouldn't expect you to suck on mine. It's just that having written about doing it in many of my books, I wondered if I would like doing it as so many men seemed to.'

My cock was really throbbing at what he had asked and wondered if it would be as good as what he had said in the book. I couldn't stop my cock from twitching as though it was bobbing the head as if nodding, to say yes.

'You…you wouldn't want me to do the same to you if I said yes?' I stammered.

'No,' he said quite emphatically. 'That is, unless you wanted to. But then you might be disappointed for there's hardly anything left in my balls. Yours look as if they hold quite a large amount of sperm.'

I looked at him but couldn't read what was in his mind, well maybe that he really did want to suck on me, but could I let him do it to me? Why not, said a voice in my head. You don't have to suck on him. You might even like it. Jerking off in his mouth instead of into some toilet paper. I didn't realise that as this voice was speaking to me that, my hand had gone down to my erection and was rubbing it. I quickly let go of it when I noticed what I was doing.

'It…it won't hurt, would it?' I stammered.

'It didn't hurt me when I was sucked on and I got a thrill at having myself cumming in the mouth on my cock and having the man swallow it,' he said in reply.

'Well,' I started to speak slowly. 'If you enjoyed it, maybe I will too,' and gave a quick look at the three houses that was close to us, 'but not here!'

'Definitely not. It would be better being comfortable on my bed. So you would like to know what it feels like in having this experience?'

'Yes grandad,' I said, my stomach feeling that it was holding a lot of butterflies inside and my heart was pounding and my cock was throbbing away not counting the shivering tingles that ran up and down my spine. 'You won't tell mum?' I couldn't help but cry out at the thought.

'No way! It would just be something kept between us,' he said as he swung his legs round and sat up. His cock was bigger than mine when erect. Not by much, and he covered himself with a towel as he stood up and wrapped it round his middle.

I did the same with my towel but it still showed that I was up hard as it poked out the front as I wrapped it round my waist and followed him up the stairs and into the house. I could feel my body trembling as we went through the kitchen and lounge and into his bedroom which was right behind the lounge and it had its own bathroom like the one upstairs.

He moved round the bed to the side which was closest to the window, and dropping his towel, he got onto the bed and lay on his side, his cock sticking out from below the paunch that he had. I was still shivering as if it was cold in the room as I dropped my towel and got onto the bed and lay next to him.

'Roll over onto your back,' he said, which I did, making my cock now lie up on my lower stomach. 'Don't forget that this is my first time of doing this and I hope that we will both enjoy the experience.' He moved down the bed a little and watched his head come down and had him kiss my stomach before raising his head to look at my cock as his hand took hold of it. His hand was warm as he lifted it upright, his fingers curling round the shaft so that the head was well clear of his hand. I could see that I had that pearly looking drop of fluid sitting over the eye of my cock and my body quivered as I saw and felt his tongue move over the head to take this drop off and into his mouth.

'Have you ever tasted this,' he asked, looking up at me, his hand still firmly holding my cock upright.

'No,' I managed to reply, my stomach all tense in spite of the butterflies inside.

'You should taste it sometime. It's nectar. Just like honey. Now for the moment of truth,' and his head went down and he took the head of my cock into his mouth. Wow! How hot the inside was as I felt his lips push down my foreskin to have his tongue move round the bare flesh. I flinched at the sudden spark that ran through me as the tip brushed against the thin piece of skin that held the foreskin to the flesh of my cock head. I learned later that this was one of the erogenous parts of the body. It gave me the tingle like you get when you put your tongue to a small battery to see if it still had some charge left in it.

I couldn't help the groan that escaped my mouth as I felt the suction of his mouth and having his tongue move round the bare flesh. His hand still had the shaft of my cock in a firm grip as it moved the covering skin slowly up and down on the covered muscle. I can't really describe all the different sensations than flowed up and down my body as his hand moved and his mouth sucked on my hard erection. It was thrilling! It was exciting and wished that I had had this done to me before as I saw his head moving up and down on my cock before I closed my eyes and let all these lovely sensations move throughout my body.

Such was the pleasure that I soon felt my sap start to rise up from my balls, knowing that I wasn't far off coming and this was much better than jerking myself off.

'I'm going to cum grandad,' I managed to say as my thighs began to tighten up and my hips started to lift themselves upwards to his head that was still moving up and down on the head of my cock. His hand held me tighter and began to move faster as he jerked me off.

'I…I'm cuming grandad, I'm…aaaah,' I groaned as the first of my emissions shot out from the eye of my cock and into his mouth, followed by another four.

His hand was now squeezing me on the upward hand movement as I gave out a sigh and felt my hips relax and sank back onto the bed. What an unforgettable experience of having him suck and still be sucking on me, feeling an extra suction as I guessed he swallowed my sperm.

It was absolutely great and his tongue was still moving round over the head as he carried on sucking for a few more minutes before finally coming to a stop and looked up at me. His eyes were actually twinkling and I'm sure that his face had a smile on it though I couldn't really tell with him still having my cock in his mouth.

'That grandad was…was fucking awesome,' I gushed. 'I didn't think it would be as good as that.' He lifted his head up off of me and I could see that the head of my cock was purple in colour and the air felt cold round it as opposed to the heat it had been in. He gave the head a kiss and looked up at me again with a big smile on his face.

'I didn't know it was going to be as good as that either,' he said, licking his lips, 'and you tasted rather nice.'

'Thank you grandad, thank you. Can I kiss you for that wonderful experience?' I said, such was the euphoria I was in and having that lovely glow in both my cock and balls. I held my arms open and he moved up the bed and into them and we kissed. I surprised myself at how passionate that kiss was, it being my first time in kissing another male person on the lips like this.

'Thank you grandad,' I said for the second time after breaking off our kiss, loving the shine in his eyes. 'It was just great. Would you like me to suck on you now?'

His eyes widened and I remember him saying down by the pool that I didn't have to suck on him in return, but now I wanted to.

'Er, you don't have to Toby,' he replied, still lying half on my upper body.

'But I want to. I want you to have the same thrill that you gave me,' I said, sure that my eyes were alight and showing the desire that I felt to make him happy with me doing it back to him.

'Well you won't get the same thrill that I felt in sucking on you,' he said. 'When you get older, the quantity of sperm being generated lessens. That is,' he chuckled, 'if I could keep it up long enough.' I looked down at him and saw that it was still erect at the moment.

'That doesn't matter. Please grandad. Let me suck on you and see if it as good as being sucked.' I said this with my heart thumping away in my chest at the very thought of sucking his cock as he had sucked on mine.

'Okay,' he said with a smile and moved himself off of me and lay down on is back, his cock looking bigger than mine laying up on his lower stomach and noticed that with him in this position, flat on his back, his paunch had disappeared. I gave his hairless chest a stroke wondering why no hair had grown there as most men did. He had hair on his arms and legs, but not there. Anyway, I gave it a stroke as I moved down the bed, looking at his circumcised cock, the head quite red and smooth.

'You've got no foreskin,' I remarked, looking at it and wondering if my mouth was big enough to take it in.

'I had that cut off quite a few years ago, but it doesn't affect what can be done with it,' I heard him say.

I was now down the bed far enough to have my face level with his groin and used my left hand to raise it up. It felt hot and hard in my hand as my fingers went round and held it firmly, feeling it throbbing away and hoped that it would stay up hard and that I would enjoy sucking on it.

I gave my lips a lick, an unconscious act before lowering my head down and took the head of his erect cock into my mouth. Wow! My mind said as I began to move my head up and down on him, letting some of my saliva coat it for easier movement. You're sucking on grandad's cock my mind shouted out at me! And it feels fucking great!

The skin that covered the shaft of his cock felt so smooth and as I began to move my hand up and down on it, it seemed to slide and move over the muscle it covered, with much ease as if there was oil inside as a form of lubrication.

'Grip it harder and move your hand faster,' I heard him say. His voice sounding as if he was much further away than lying under my shoulder. This I did as I started using my tongue to move round the head of his bare cock and heard him groan at each sweep that I made round it, not knowing then that it was crossing over the G string to make him give out a shiver beneath me.

I now found that I was enjoying this, sucking on his cock and having him give out little moans as I jerked away as I sucked and tongued him.

'I'm not far off Toby,' I heard him say. 'Grip it harder and move faster…for I'm…cumming.' And I felt the head of his cock swell a little bit more and I had some of his cum spurt into my mouth. Not a lot, but at least there was some, and as he said, not a lot. But it was there and I could move it round the head with my tongue as I kept on sucking and had it slide down my throat while I did so. His thigh under my left arm had tensed up as he began to cum and now I felt it soften as he relaxed his body at having had an emission and I felt quite proud of myself for having sucked and swallowed his sperm.

The strength of his cock suddenly started to soften too and knew that this was the end of this first sucking of another man's cock and I licked all 'round the head before finally letting it slip out of my mouth to look up at grandad. He had a big smile on his face and I think I had the same as he opened his arms and I moved back up the bed and lay on top of him as I went in between them and we kissed.

'That was awesome grandad,' I gushed when we broke off the kiss which was quite passionate, his arms still round my back as he held me there. I could feel his heart beating and reverberating against my chest much as I mine did against his. 'Just like you've written in the book. It was great!' He pulled my head down for another kiss. 'When can we do it again?' I asked him, freeing my mouth from his and looking down into his shining eyes.

'Later, for my stomach is telling me that it needs food. You can help in getting lunch,' he said, releasing me from his arms. I watched the way his flaccid cock moved as he got off the bed and found that I really wanted to suck it again and have him suck mine. It disappeared from my sight as he turned to the dresser and opened a drawer and pulled out two pieces of cloth.

'Here,' he said, throwing one to me which I caught as I got off the bed. 'It's a sarong which is what I normally wear all the time during the summer. You just wrap it round your middle and tuck the ends in. It's just in case you spill something while cooking,' and gave a little laugh. 'There are parts of the body that we don't want to get burnt or scalded.'

I knew what parts he was talking about and grinned back at him as I copied his way of fixing it round my waist. I followed him from the bedroom and through the lounge to the kitchen where we prepared lunch.

CHAPTER III

After lunch we went back down to the pool. 'Only an hour in the sun Toby,' he said as I stretched out on the lounger. 'Take the sarong off and lay on your front so that I can put some sun block on your back. Let's give you a safe sun tan.'

I wriggled about in getting the sarong off and had grandad pour some lotion on my back and had him rub it all over my back and legs. I got a funny tingle inside as I felt his hand rub it over the cheeks of my bum and started to get an erection at the softness of his hand moving over that part of my body.

'That'll do you for an hour. Here, have a beer,' and passed me a can, surprising me at giving me this drink. I popped it open and took a swig and then put the can down and carried on reading the book I had started last night. On reading where I left off, I began to have my cock getting hard pressed up against my stomach and had to put the book down as I was really now uncomfortable. I lay there and thought back to the morning in grandad's bedroom and wanted him to suck on me again, and, and then suck on his too.

I must have dozed off for quite some time and woke up and found that he had shifted the umbrella and I was now in the shade. I finished the beer which was now quite warm and slipped off the lounger and dived into the pool. My back had felt a bit sore but the water cooled me down all over. It was nice to swim up and down that small pool and I realised at how happy I was to now be with my grandad.

=oOo=

I had nearly an hour in the pool before he called me out as it was time for us to get dinner. I now had no compunction or shyness at getting out of the pool and stand naked before him as I dried myself before putting the sarong back on round my waist to follow him up the stairs into the house.

While dinner was cooking, I went back down and collected the empty beer cans, towels and the book and tidied up down there. I was even given another can of beer when I returned and drank this while we had dinner.

'How's your back?' grandad asked me.

'Fine. It tingles a bit but okay,' I said.

'Tomorrow you can get some sun on your front,' he said. It was the word front that triggered my mind off to what I had at the front. Well what he had too.

'Grandad,' I began, wondering what he would think at what I was going to ask with us having finished eating. 'Er, grandad. Can we, er, go to bed now, for I want to suck on you and have you suck on me again?'

There! I had said it and I'm sure my face was red at asking for this again and felt that I had a hard on and hoped he would say yes.

'I don't see why not,' he said, and my heart gave a leap. 'For there's fuck all on the t.v.' I couldn't help but give him a grin and stood up and his eyes went straight down to the front of my sarong to see that I had tented it. He then smiled and stood up and I saw that he was in the same state as me with having an erection at the thought of us sucking each other again. 'We can do the dishes in the morning,' he said, still with that smile on his face as he offered me his hand which I took and let him lead me to the bedroom.

Both our sarongs fell to the floor as we got onto the bed and he leaned over me and kissed me on the lips. It was a lovely kiss, and the thought struck me that it seemed like the kind of kiss one would give to a lover. Was he falling in love with me for I sure as hell was falling in love with him. Grandfather or not, I was sure that I was and gave him back the same kind of kiss that he had just given me.

He then kissed my chin, throat and chest as he slowly moved down the bed, stopping at my nipples and kissed each one with a little nibble at them, making them stand up quite hard and giving me an inner thrill at him doing this. He carried on kissing his way down my body, poking his tongue into the indentation of my stomach before moving his tongue further down until it was moving over the half exposed head of my erect cock.

I couldn't help the shiver that ran through at the touch of his tongue once again on my cock, taking off the clear pearl white drop of dew that had come out of the eye. His eyes flashed up at me, shining brightly before he bent his head and took me into the heat of his mouth, lifting my cock upright as he did so. I gave out a gasp as I felt that heat and of him pushing the foreskin down as he then began to suck on me again. I was in heaven at feeling his tongue move over the bare flesh and making me quiver when he hit the G string, loving what he was doing and the thrill at the same time.

His right arm was on my thigh as his hand took hold of the shaft of my cock and began moving it up and down as before, holding it firm and not too tight as he moved the soft skin up and down over the muscle that it covered while he kept on with his sucking of me. I couldn't help but give out a groan at the pleasure I was getting of his tongue stroking the bare flesh, his hand moving up and down on my shaft and then wondered why he changed hands.

I soon found out as he shifted his body a little and then had the shock of having that free hand now cup my balls and start moving them around in their little bag. This evinced another groan from me at this new pleasure he was giving me as that hand gently squeezed each one in turn, giving them something like a massage. With this extra erotic sensation, my body started to react and he must have felt my body tensing up for he gripped my cock tighter and began moving his hand faster, not slowing down in his sucking.

My hips started lifting themselves up to technically fuck his mouth as I felt the first surge of my sperm move up and erupt into his hot mouth. My clenched fist beat a tattoo on the bed as more of my seed was ejected out of the eye to join the first salvo and I let go at least another three if not four before I felt completely drained in all of my senses at that wonderful feeling of lassitude as my body relaxed from the pleasure I had just been given by grandad.

I felt that extra suction on the head of my cock and knew that he had just swallowed my emissions and knew now that grandad did love me, why else would he have sucked on my cock, played with my balls and swallowed my sperm? He gave my cock a few more jerks, squeezing the head to get the last of my semen out before he lifted his head up, letting me feel the cool air cover the head as he licked round the bare flesh and gave the tip a kiss before letting go and moving up the bed to lie on his back next to me.

I rolled over to lie on top of him and his arms came up round my back as I kissed him for the pleasure he had just given me.

'I love you grandad,' I breathed out between my kisses.

'I love you too Toby,' he said, his eyes bright and looking into mine which I'm sure mirrored his in this declaration from both of us.

'Do you want me to suck on you now?' I asked, although I felt that his cock was still rather soft lying next to my still hard one, both being squashed between our stomachs. He gave a little snort.

'I wouldn't bother Toby,' he said rolling me off of him. 'You wouldn't get any joy out of it as it is at the moment. Just let me stroke your body for it is in a much better condition than mine was at your age.'

I didn't object and had his hand move down my chest to the upper-thigh before coming back up, moving across my now deflating cock. He stroked my arms, my flat stomach and even fondled my balls as I lay lethargic and almost comatose in enjoyment of having his hand rove over my body.

He moved his body on the bed and his head came down to mine and he kissed me. Not only on the lips, but my chin and throat, and moving his body round as his kisses came to my nipples, that he gave little nips at before carrying on down to my stomach, nearly being upside down to me. The kisses carried on to my cock where he also used his tongue that then stroked the underside of my cock, giving that nibbles as well and then had the pleasant jolt of having him take my balls into his mouth.

It was then I realised why he had turned round on the bed for I had the tip of his cock that I could feel now up hard, pressing against my cheek, so it was easy to just turn my head and take the head into my mouth. It wasn't the best of positions in doing this and slowly and gently moved my body onto my side, having to move slow so that he didn't chew my balls off with my moving.

Now I understood the expression I had heard of before of having sex in the sixty-nine position. He was sucking on my balls as I sucked on the head of his cock. With me now lying on my side, it was easy to bring my left hand up and hold the shaft of his now hard cock and rub it up and down as I sucked on the bare flesh of the head.

I only did this for a few minutes but then released him, nipping the underside of his cock with my teeth as I went down lower to then take his balls into my mouth to be doing the same to him as he was doing to me. I slowly rolled them round in my mouth feeling that they took up more space than the head of his cock as I sucked them.

'Your balls feel bigger than mine,' I said after briefly releasing them from my mouth, before taking them back inside to continue moving them around as I sucked. I felt him release mine.

'They're a lot older than yours,' he said before taking them back into the heat of his mouth. We carried on like this for several minutes, during which, my cock had become fully erect again and so he released my balls and pulled my cock up and took the head into his mouth to start sucking on that. I copied him as he was still hard and wondered if he had the same amount of sperm inside him as last time though I would like to have had more than that to get a proper taste of him.

It didn't take long of his sucking and jerking my cock before I began to spray and fill his mouth with my seed that came out of my cock and had the joy of having him do the same to me. The pleasure was that there was more than last time and I had enough to move it round with my tongue to get the taste, which wasn't unpleasant, before swallowing it as he did to mine. Though as soon as he had come, his cock began to soften until I was able to have the whole length of it inside my mouth and my nose buried in his pubic hairs.

I gently chewed on it like it was a soft rubber bone that one gives to a dog to chew and play with, though I didn't bark, I gave out little sounds of pleasure as I did this. He eventually gave up the squeezing of my cock having completely emptied me and felt the kiss he gave to the head and pulled his out of my mouth and turned round on the bed and up to cuddle me to his chest for us to kiss each other once again.

We both lay in each other's arms, gently stroking the flesh beneath our hands as we slowly kissed, using our tongues too, to play with each other before I broke of the kissing and nestled my head into his shoulder, feeling rather tired now.

'Can I sleep with you grandad? I feel so comfortable here,' I mumbled.

'Of course you can Toby. It's been a long time since I was able to cuddle someone before falling asleep,' he said, his voice sounding tired like mine had, and so that's where I slept that night and for the rest of my stay with him.

=oOo=

'That's nice,' I groaned as I came awake with grandad sucking on the head of my cock and with him now knowing I was awake, lifted my cock upright and I felt my foreskin being pushed down by his lips and had my body twitch as his tongue caught my G string. He stopped and felt him moving himself on the bed. 'Don't stop now grandad,' I moaned. Still not having opened my eyes and felt his hot breath first before he engulfed the head again to my sigh as he began sucking and teasing me once more.

It didn't take long before I began to buck my hips and his hand began to move faster as I then erupted into his mouth, giving him the fresh semen that had generated themselves inside my balls overnight. My last two shots were not exactly that, for his suction was more like a vacuum cleaner in pulling it out of me, clearing the tube. Oh God, I loved my grandad with him taking me to heaven with what he was doing to and for me. He finished with licking all over the head before kissing the top and giving me a big smile.

As I've already said, it was a lovely way of being woken up and as we were both now wide awake, it was time to get up and see the teeth brushing, shower and having either just a pee or that and a crap. With our ablutions finished, we put on our sarongs and went and both worked together in seeing to our breakfast.

'One of the best times for sunbathing,' grandad said when we went down to the pool. 'The morning sun and the other is when it is going down. Now roll onto your back and let me put some sun cream on you.' This I did with a grin which he returned knowing that he would spend quite a bit of his time in stroking my cock as he put the oil on me. Even this was sensuous as he stroked the oil over my body and I even moved my legs apart for him to even coat my balls.

He finished and wiped his hand on his towel as I gave a stretch and settled down for that hour in catching the sun. I had that hour before he told me to move the umbrella to cover myself and there I stayed for another hour before we both went into the pool where I did quite a few laps up and down the pool with him sitting on that underwater bench to watch me. That was it till it was lunch time which was really only a snack before we were back down by the pool.

With the umbrella giving us shade, I carried on reading my book and didn't know that he was looking at me as I got an erection at what I was reading.

'I see that it's turning you on,' grandad said looking at my cock sticking out from my thighs.

'Yes. He's in the middle of fucking his mate,' I said, going slightly red in the face at him seeing me get this erection again from reading one of his books.

'That will be Marcus fucking Tracey then,' he said, and I turned the book cover towards me and saw that he had noticed the title.

'Yes and both of them are loving it,' I said and saw him lick his lips.

'Would you like to be Marcus if I was Tracey,' grandad asked me in a soft voice. I was stunned! Did I hear him right? He wanted to play out what was in the book? Him really asking me if I wanted to fuck him?

'You…you mean that you would let me do the same as they are doing in the book?' I stammered, looking to see what kind of look he had on his face.

'Well I've never played the part of Tracey before, but there's always the first time and you look capable enough,' grandad said.

'I…you…you'll let me fuck you, you mean?' I stammered again, somewhat incredulously, looking at him.

'Yes. That is if you want to? I don't think you've ever fucked anybody before, so it would be a first for both of us for I've never had an erect cock pushed up into me, so we'll both learn something,' he said.

'I…I haven't yet as you said grandad, but, well, if you wouldn't mind,' I managed to get out with a stutter.'

'Shall we go inside and try it?' grandad said with a gentle smile and he sat up and swung his legs off the lounger and could see that he had an erection. Seeing it swing about between his thighs gave me food for thought.

'Would…would it mean that if I fucked you, you would want to fuck me afterwards?' I asked in a trembling voice, feeling butterflies once again fluttering around in my stomach.

'No Toby,' he said. 'It might be hard now but it won't stay like that. It never does and it soon deflates.'

He took his sarong and covered himself as he stood up. So I put the book down and got my sarong and got up, covering myself in the same way. I felt myself trembling as I followed him upstairs and on into his bedroom where he opened the drawer on his side of the bed and brought out a pot of what looked like cream. This he put down and took off his sarong and got onto the bed. I then took my sarong off and got onto the bed, my cock really throbbing now and swung between my legs, not knowing whether to lay down or not so just sat there with it sticking up from my groin.

'You've really got a lovely looking cock Toby,' grandad said as he took hold of the pot of cream and took off the lid. 'It looks even bigger now and maybe too much for me to take in, so let's use a bit of cream to help.'

He dipped his finger into the pot and scooped out some and smeared it over the head of my erection and then got some more out and his hand disappeared behind him and guessed he was putting it where my cock was going to go. He put the pot back on the side and turning round, got up onto his knees and leaned forward on the bed, resting his upper body on his forearms with his backside up in the air.

'Well you've read the book so you know what to do,' grandad said, 'but take it slow for you've got a big cock and it will probably hurt a bit before you are fully inside me. So go slow. Take it easy.'

I'm sure my face was red as I got up onto my knees and shuffled myself round, lifting each knee at a time as I got over his legs which he had spread apart. With my right hand holding onto his hip, got myself into position and saw, with his legs far apart which had opened up the crease between the cheeks of his bum and I could see the blob of cream that was my target. So holding my cream covered cock with my left hand, I moved in closer and felt him flinch when the head touched where my cock was going to go.

Using my body weight to hold it there, took hold of his other hip and took a deep breath and slowly began to ease my hips forward, feeling the resistance of his ring piece. As grandad had said, I slowly kept up the pressure and saw the cream parting and the head of my cock starting to be compressed a little as it started to slowly enter his backside.

'Relax yourself,' I heard grandad grunt as I kept up the pressure and suddenly, the head of my cock was inside his ass. There was a whoosh of breath that came from his mouth and I felt the heat of his insides and I'm sure it was that hot that it was melting the cream. 'Christ! That hurt!' grandad exclaimed.

'Do you want me to pull out?' I asked of him, leaning slightly over his rear end.

'No! No! It's alright now. The pain is easing. Just take it slow for your cock feels bigger than it looks,' he panted and I could hear him taking in deep breaths. I slowly pushed up to him and so the shaft of my cock started to disappear and could now feel that muscle inside flexing away round my cock as I was pushing it further inside his ass. I lost sight of it as my thighs came up tight to the cheeks of his bum and I could go no further and he let out another big gasp and sighed.

'Does it still hurt?' I asked of him.

'No, no, it's okay now and easing off now that you are fully inside and it feels great. I can feel it throbbing,' he said. That's when it hit me that I actually had my cock up his ass and was about to fuck him. I thought it was great too, feeling the heat all round my cock and having it constantly being squeezed by his muscle in that tight orifice. This gave me a great thrill that I was now having my first fuck, albeit up a man's backside, but what the fuck! It was a hole that my cock liked being in and so began to slowly move myself back and forth. Loving the feel of the compression all round my cock as I moved, holding his hips in a firm grasp.

What heaven this was to be moving my cock in such a tight place and really settled down to give him as much pleasure as I was getting in the fucking of my grandad.

'This is great,' grandad panted out. 'I can feel every inch of you. It's fantastic!'

'No pain then?' I panted, still moving myself in and out of his backside.

'No. That's gone,' said, his voice muffled slightly and saw that he was face down into the pillow. 'Keep going and let me feel you cum.'

Which wasn't long and found that I was nearly there and so held his hips tighter as I began to pull him back onto my forward thrusts and I reached that peak and my cock started to really throb and I held the cheeks of his bum tight up to my thighs as my hips began to jerk and I shot my first load up into his ass.

'I felt that Toby,' he cried out as I sent more and more up into him and realised that I was crooning as I came inside him until it was all gone and I came to a stop. I leaned over his rear end, panting away as my cock still kept throbbing away inside him. I could feel that my chest was covered in sweat as I took in deep breaths as grandad gave out a gurgling noise and had his muscle squeezing me like mad as though he was trying to milk me to get more semen out of my cock.

I eased myself up straight and began to pull out, watching my cock slowly emerge from his back side, his muscle now gripping me tight as though trying to hold me there, but out I came and sat back on my heels to see some cream still round the shaft of it as it was still up hard sticking out from my groin. Grandad slump forward as I just sat there musing that I had just fucked my first man. In fact it was my first fuck.

'What a wonderful fuck Toby,' he panted as he now lay down fully on the bed. 'Now go and wash yourself, thoroughly, making sure that your foreskin is pulled right back.'

I slowly rose up onto my knees again and worked my way to the edge of the bed and got off and couldn't help but stagger a little as my legs felt like rubber. I made my way into the bathroom and got my cock over the edge of the basin and turned on the tap and carefully washed myself as he had said. This done, I took a towel off the rail and dried myself, my cock still fairly hard before going back into the bedroom to see grandad now lying on his side with the biggest grin I'd seen so far on his face as he patted the bed next to him.

'That was incredible grandad,' I said as I got on next to him and went into his open arms. 'Thank you,' and we kissed. Boy what a kiss it was too. Open mouthed and with an incredible amount of passion it was as he kissed me. This kissing lasted for quite some time and I loved every minute of it until we finally broke off, both of us breathing rather heavily.

I could feel that he was still a little hard and so slid down the bed and took the head of his cock into my mouth to suck and tease him with my tongue. As much as I sucked and chewed on him, I couldn't raise it up any harder and so after a few more minutes of trying, gave up and moved back up into his arms for some more kisses.

'Can I fuck you again tonight in bed here grandad?' I asked. He smiled at me.

'Of course you can Toby. I loved having you massage my back passage. You must have enjoyed it too.'

'That I did grandad. That's why I'd like to do it again,' I said with a grin on my face.

'Well we'd better get something to eat. We've got to keep your strength up haven't we,' he said with a smile. So we got off the bed and put our sarongs on and went to find what we could eat.

CHAPTER IV

It was a light lunch again and we spent the afternoon down by the pool. Grandad rubbed sun cream on my back as I lay on the lounger and I'm sure his hand lingered more on the cheeks of my bum than any other part of my body. He wanted me to get as brown as him but to still be careful and would only let me lie in the sun for an hour. We did some swimming too, me flying up and down the length of the pool while he did leisurely back strokes until it was time for dinner. My body by now was quite red in most parts but there were shades of brown that showed it wouldn't be long before I was brown all over.

I gave grandad a hand in preparing our evening meal, getting better in my cooking under his tutelage, well, I had to pay him back by helping him in doing some of the chores. It didn't take long with two of us doing it and we both enjoyed the finished product. With it over and the things all washed up and put away, grandad suggested watching a DVD on the television, and it was in a shy voice that I answered him.

'I'd rather go to bed,' I said. He nodded in agreement and we went off to the bedroom where we discarded our sarongs and got on the bed.

'Do you want me to put some soothing cream on your back?' grandad asked as we settled down.

'There's only one place I want the cream,' I said, hoping that it was more of a smile and not a smirk.

'Later. Let's have a little fun first,' grandad said as he began to stroke my erection and went and turned round on the bed so that I had his half erect cock in front of me and when he took the head of my cock into his mouth, I took his into mine. I was quite proud that with my sucking on him, managed to bring it up to be hard and even had him come in my mouth to savour before swallowing. Though what I got was nowhere the amount that I gave him, emptying my balls for him to taste and then swallow. We kept on sucking till we both deflated and he turned round for us to kiss and use our hands to stroke as much of each other's body as we could.

It only took me just under the hour before with him stroking my cock as well as fondling my balls, I was once again sporting an erection. With me being up hard again, he let go of me and turned and fumbled in the bedside drawer and pulled out a square wrapper. With this being torn open, he produced what he said was a condom, a rubber that should really always be worn when having anal sex. He told me that it was some years ago that my mother had given him a bag full, but have never got round to having had to use one.

He gave the head of my cock a brief suck before he began to roll it down over my erection.

'Do I have to wear this grandad?' I said as he did this.

'Well it does have its advantages. One, it stops me getting pregnant,' which made both of us laugh. 'Second, you don't have to get off out of bed to wash yourself, and third. I can strip it off and suck out any semen left inside your cock.'

It seemed strange to see my cock covered in this protective rubber but guessed that he was right though the first bit was rather stupid, that being the little bit at the end that collected the sperm. The pot of cream had been left on the bedside table so as grandad turned round on the bed, assuming the position on his hands and knees, I took some cream out of the pot and smeared over the head of my covered cock and a blob between the cheeks of his bum.

'Take it slow and gently,' he said, 'until I'm comfortable with it inside me.'

Grandad had said this as I was getting behind and in between his legs and with one hand holding my covered cock straight, placed it in the center of the blob of cream that concealed the entrance to his tight cave, making him flinch again. I did as he asked and slowly began to push myself inside his ass, feeling the resistance of his muscle as the head of my cock was being compressed as it began to move inside to once again feel his inner body heat. It was lovely holding his hips, knowing that I was going to have immense pleasure in fucking him again.

With the head suddenly being inside, I stopped for a moment until I felt he was ready for me to carry on and I remembered an old cowboy song, well only the first line and so crooned "Back in the saddle again", which made grandad grunt, though if it was because I was making his canal wider or my crooning, I don't know, but it was lovely having this tight fit completely surrounding my cock as I slid inside him. It was just like fitting a finger in a glove it was that tight.

He gave out a big sigh when I came to a stop with my thighs up tight to the cheeks of his bum, my cock throbbing away inside him, almost in tune with his muscle constantly flexing itself round my shaft. It was lovely holding his hips and moving myself back and forth inside him, getting a grand thrill in the doing of this, making love to him in this fashion. Love! Where did that word spring from my mind cried out? Well you love fucking your grandad, the voice said. True, I replied to the voice in my head. I did love fucking him and in this short space of time of knowing him, guessed that I was falling in love with him.

'Harder, Toby! Harder,' I heard him say, and so I did just that and began ramming myself up tight to his bum and felt my balls smacking his upper legs. It didn't take long before I was pulling his hips back onto me as I thrust myself up into him, loving the little grunts he kept giving out and then I straightened up my back and let my hips do all the moving as I began to shoot my load up into the condom.

I found that I was panting heavily as I came to a stop, leaning over his back, my cock still throbbing away inside him, really finding out how exhausting it was in fucking a man up the ass. Feeling my strength returning, I straightened up and began pulling out, feeling his muscle straining itself round my still hard shaft and finally came out to little cries from him.

I had barely sat back on my heels before he was turning round on the bed and with some tissues in his hand, pulled the condom off me to drop it all on the floor before lying down and taking the head of my cock into his mouth. I had seen when the condom had come off of me, that the head was coated with some of my sperm and now he was licking this off prior to sucking on me to drag out any sperm left inside my cock. His hand was constantly squeezing me on the upward stroke of his hand and felt the pressure he was creating as he did so.

He eventually let go of me and turned back round on the bed and opened his arms for me to fall into and we then kissed as he cuddled me. It was in this cuddle we stayed until we both finally dropped off to sleep.

=oOo=

I came awake in the morning feeling on top of the world lying there next to grandad and saw that he had woken up too and I smiled at him and rolled over to half lay on top of him, my morning erection pressed up against his thigh.

'I love you grandad,' I said with my mouth on his to then kiss him before laying my head down on his chest as his arms held me.

'I love you too Toby' he said, his voice a little thick as he stroked my back. With him doing this, I moved my hand down and found that his cock was up and hard and I curled my fingers round it and began to rub it.

'You're up and hard grandad,' I said and worked my way out of his arms and slithered down the bed and took the head of his cock into my mouth. He gave out a groan and wondered if my mouth felt as hot as his with it fully inside for me to run my tongue over the bare flesh as I sucked at the same time. It was throbbing away and gave little jerks as my tongue touched the G string and felt his body start to stiffen up. I held the shaft of his cock in a tighter grasp and moved it faster and was rewarded by feeling the head expand a little and had his hips buck up towards my mouth as I felt his sperm come up the inside of his cock and erupt into my mouth. There wasn't much of it but enough for me to move round in my mouth before swallowing it and sucking even harder to get any more that might still be inside. I eventually released him and gave the head a kiss before slowly moving up his body, covering it with kisses, even the nipples on his chest and giving them a nip or two before I reached his face and kissed him on the lips.

'I tasted you this time grandad,' I said, breaking off the kiss to see his big smile. 'Not a lot, but it was alright. Will you suck on me now?'

'Gladly,' he said and eased me off of him so that I was flat on my back, my erection lying up on my stomach, throbbing away at the expectation of being sucked again. He kissed me first on the lips before moving down and kissing each nipple and sucking them too for a few minutes before carrying on down kissing my stomach until he felt the head of my cock brush his cheek.

I then got the thrill again of him taking me into his hot mouth, just loving the way his tongue moved over the bare flesh after he had pushed the foreskin right back with his lips. The exquisite tingle that ran through my body as he licked the G string, making me tremble and my balls begin to ache, his hand gently moving the skin of my cock up and down. He moved his body further round and opened my legs for him to be comfortable as he continued sucking and licking me, but then lifted his head up off and looked up at me.

'Put your hands round my head and face fuck me Toby,' he said, taking me back into his mouth. His hand gripped the base end of my shaft as I put both hands to the side of his head and he stopped bobbing his head up and down as I began lifting my hips in the same action and gave him what he called a face fuck. His hand prevented me from getting the whole length of my cock into his mouth which might have choked him as I bucked away, his lips tight round the head of my cock, feeling his teeth scrape the flesh.

'I'm cumming grandad...I... I'm cumming,' I gasped out as I felt my seed boiling and begin to move up the tube that runs up the underside of my cock and had the release that I needed as I came shooting out all that my balls had generated into his waiting mouth. It didn't seem to stop pumping out and lost count of how many shots I had, such was the pleasure of once again giving him my semen to taste and savour before swallowing it. This he did as my hips stopped lifting up from the bed and I gave out a sigh as he continued for another couple of minutes, squeezing the head of my cock as he sucked the last out of me before licking the head clean and giving the head its usual kiss before really letting go of me.

'Oh grandad. That was awesome!' I cried as I pulled at his head to come back up the bed for me to kiss him.

'I enjoyed it too,' he said, breaking off the kiss, 'but it's time for breakfast for I'm hungry to put something else in my mouth.'

'I'll cook breakfast,' I said, rolling out from under him and scooting off into the bathroom. I didn't bother with having a shower but just a quick wash of my face and the brushing of my teeth before grabbing my sarong and going off to the kitchen. I don't know what took him so long for I had cooked the eggs, bacon and fried tomatoes with some slices of toast all ready and was just putting it on the dining table when he showed up wearing his sarong.

CHAPTER V

With breakfast over and the things washed up, I got another book from his office and we went down to the pool where he covered my body again with sun cream, seeing that my body was already starting to be a lovely shade of brown. I also loved to feel his hands moving over me as he rubbed the oil over my bum, cock and balls.

I laid there in the sun reading and it wasn't long before I had an erection and wasn't really aware of me doing what I was with it until grandad spoke.

'Would you like me to do that?' he asked, startling me for I had been so engrossed in the book. I gave him a smile.

'I'd rather use it somewhere else than in your hand,' I said, and got a grin back.

'You're really a randy fucker,' he said as his grin widened, 'and I don't mind at all.' He sat up and picked up his sarong before standing up and wrapping it round his waist. I put my book down and quickly did the same and then followed him up the stairs and into the house, heading off to the bedroom.

'Use a condom so that I can suck on you afterwards,' he said as he dropped his sarong and got onto the bed. I took mine off and got a condom out of its wrapper and quickly rolled it down over my throbbing erection before taking a scoop of cream from the pot and covering the head and some where he wanted it, right where my condom clad cock was going to go.

He was on his hands and knees, well I should say forearms for he was leaning the top half of his body right down so that his shoulders were touching the bed. This position making his bum stick right up in the air. I quickly got in between his legs, my cock bouncing about so much that I had to hold it to be able to hit the target that I'd creamed ready.

Doing as I'd been told before, I took it slow and watched the head slowly disappear and then felt the heat and his muscle trying to grip me, but with the cream, it was unable to stop me from carrying on and had my cock slide nicely up into his ass. There wasn't a grunt this time, only a big sigh when my thighs came up tight to the cheeks of his bum. For some reason I had been holding my breath as I entered him and now let it out and took another deep breath as I began to move myself inside his canal.

'That's nice Toby,' he breathed out as I slowly fucked him. 'It's so soothing.'

'You like me fucking you grandad?' I asked, not stopping my steady in and out movement of my prick up his ass.

'You wouldn't believe the pleasure it gives you as your cock smoothness out the wrinkles inside and the thrill of it just being there,' he panted. It thrilled my heart that he loved me doing this to him and so I would fuck him as much as I was able during my holiday with him. But the pleasure is short lived as nature takes over and I knew I wasn't far off of cumming inside him. So holding his hips firmly, I began to really plough his field and had him start to grunt with every forward push and moved faster until I began shooting my sperm into, albeit the condom, but it didn't make any difference to me. I finally came to a stop having given him all that I had to give and leaned over his rear end, drops of my sweat falling onto his back and had to shake my head for it was rolling down my forehead and into my eyes.

He gave out a little cry as I pulled out and sat back on my heels and he was quick to turn round and pull the condom off of me to take the head of my cock into his mouth to suck out any semen left. He only did this for a few minutes before releasing me and rolling over onto his back beside me. As he was now upside down to me, it was easy to move up from my heels and stretch myself half on top of him and take his cock into my mouth. It was semi hard but enough for me to gently chew on the rubbery head while I sucked on him and then using my tongue to tease the G string. But with it steadily deflating, it didn't seem to be much fun at not arousing him to come in my mouth and so gave up and let him go to roll over onto my back. He then turned round and gave me a cuddle as he kissed my cheek.

'I like sucking on your cock grandad and love it when you suck mine. I also like fucking you and you seem to enjoy me doing it too,' I said to him.

'I do Toby, I do. It's a wonderful feeling having you moving inside me and really enjoy you fucking me,' he said, squeezing me in his arms.

'Er...well...er, as you like it so much, will you let me have the experience?' There! I'd said it now, the thought having been in the back of my mind. 'Will...you fuck me?' My body all of a sudden tremble at having asked him to do this. Would he? My heart was thumping away in my chest as I waited for his answer.

'Are you sure you want me to Toby,' he slowly said, a serious look on his face.

'Yes grandad. I would like to know just how much you enjoy it,' I replied.

'I don't know if I can keep it up hard long enough,' he said.

'We can only try, even if it's only for a minute or two,' I said, my heart really hammering away inside me.

'Okay, but it will have to be later this afternoon for it's no good at the moment,' and I looked down to see that he was right, for his cock was soft and no way would he be able to give me the experience of having it up inside me in its present state.

'I can see that,' I said somewhat petulantly at not being able to have him fuck me straight away, mind you, I was in the same state having mine as soft as his, so we left the bedroom and went down to have a swim before lunch.

=oOo=

We'd had lunch and just finished doing the washing up when I spoke what was in my mind. 'Can we go to bed now grandad?' I'm sure my voice was like that of a small boy in asking that question. My cock was throbbing away and poking out the front of my sarong.

'What for?' he asked with a straight look on his face.

'I…I want you to fuck me,' I stammered, feeling my face get hot. 'I…I want to know what it's like. You seem to enjoy it, don't you?'

'I must admit that I do though I never thought that I would,' he replied.

'Well it looks as though you would like to fuck me,' I said, pointedly looking down to see that he was tenting his sarong the same as I was.

'Okay,' he said with a grin that lit my face up, so I went straight off to the bedroom with him following me this time and in there, got the pot of cream and two condoms out of the drawer and put them on the side.

'Will…will you fuck me first grandad,' I stammered, dropping my sarong and getting onto the bed. He grinned and nodded his head as his sarong came off and I saw that he had a nice looking erect cock that in a minute or two would have pushed up inside me. I was trembling as he got on the bed next to me and I was now having huge butterflies churning themselves up in my stomach.

'I think that I'd better help to make it a bit easier first,' he said, reaching for the pot of cream.

'How?' I asked.

'By using my fingers to, er, widen you a little, otherwise it would really hurt with it being the first time,' he said.

'I didn't use my fingers with you the first time,' I said.

'No. That's because I er, knew a little bit more about this, having used er, a vibrator before,' he said, his face now a little red in saying this.

'You've got a vibrator?' I asked. 'Can I see it. I've heard of them but never seen one.'

'It's er, in the top drawer there,' he said. I was on what would be his side of the bed at this moment, and so rolled over and opened the drawer. 'At the back.' I rummaged through odd bits and pieces and found a slender tube that was made of what looked like steel but was lighter than that material and brought it out and held it in my hand. It was about eight inches long but not very wide and had a plastic base that, as he told me, you twisted it, which I did and had it suddenly vibrating in my hand, him saying that it had two batteries inside.

'Can we use this too?' I asked, my stomach churning at the thought of having it vibrate inside of me instead of in my hand as it was doing now.

'Okay,' he laughed, taking it from me and turning it off. 'Lay on your back and lift your legs up.' This I did as he put the top of the vibrator into the pot of cream to coat it and he moved down the bed a little with it in his hand.

I flinched a little as I felt the cold cream touch the entrance to my backside and I felt him moving it round in his hand as he slowly pushed it into my ass. I got a thrill at feeling it enter me and move up a little way as he then turned the base knob and it began to vibrate.

'Oooh,' I cried. 'It feels funny. But it's nice,' as he moved it about inside me, up and down and even sideways for my insides to feel the fast pulsating thing really get me excited.

'There's a big difference between this and the real thing,' he said as he slowly moved it up and down inside me.

'Yes?' I panted. Loving the thrill I was getting from it.

'One is that not many males have a cock eight or more inches in length as this thing is. Two. My cock, again like most men is only about six and half inches long. Three. This vibrator is just under an inch in circumference whereas I, again like most, is about two inches. That's why I should use my fingers to widen you a little bit more.'

I gave out a cry when he pulled it out and turned it off. My legs came back down to the bed as he cleaned the cream off with some tissues before putting it to one side.

'Lay on your side facing me,' he said as he got some cream onto his index finger. This I did and he came up close to me and began to kiss me. I returned the kiss by putting my arm round his shoulder and felt him nudge my leg which I raised up over his thigh.

Then I felt his finger push up into my backside and gave out a shiver as it went in as far as it could. This was moved around as we kissed and it was pulled out and we broke off the kiss as he now creamed two fingers and back to kissing again as I had these two pushed up into my ass.

There was a big difference now at having them both move in different ways and also felt him trying to spread then to make my asshole wider. This was okay but there was a little pain when it came to having three fingers up my ass, being moved and wiggled around until he couldn't widen me any more with them, and so he pulled them out and wiped the excess cream off with some tissues.

'The secret is to relax, Toby. Relax your body, especially your sphincter muscle. You'll find it difficult at first but try, try to keep relaxed,' he told me as he rolled the condom down over his erect cock before putting quite a bit of cream on the top. 'Okay. Onto your knees then,' he said, which I did with some trepidation, spreading my legs and leaning forward onto my forearms as grandad got behind me. I couldn't help the flinch my body gave out at the touch of the cold cream to my ring piece. I was really trembling now as a hand came to my hip and felt the head of his cock get settled at the entrance into me.

'Relax Toby, relax,' he said in a soft voice. 'If it is too painful, which will be a little at this first time, tell me to stop if it gets too much,' and I felt him start to slowly push his cock up into me. I couldn't stop my inside muscle from trying to prevent the entry, feeling the head slowly forcing its way in, pain starting to be felt as it made me wider and yet wider.

'Relax Toby!' he said in a more authoritative way.

I was now gritting my teeth at the pain I was feeling and suddenly gave a jump as I felt his free hand suddenly slap the cheek of my bum. I had almost reached the point of asking him to stop, but with this slap, the head was suddenly inside me. Wow! Was it really throbbing or not. Nowhere near as fast as the vibrator but had much more of a feeling to it as we were like statues at this moment, not moving at all, except for the head of his cock with its throbbing away inside me. It was an incredible feeling that got even better as he began again to slowly push himself into me, the pain now just a dull throb as he slowly began to fill me with is lovely organ that was playing a rhythm that I had never felt before.

My face was burning and suddenly gasped, not realising that I had been holding my breath and my heart was thumping away in my chest and it heaved as I took in more air into my lungs. But still his cock was slowly filling me, expanding me a little every time and my muscle there flexing itself away at the intrusion. It wasn't until I felt his thighs up against my bum cheeks that I knew he was in as far as he was going to and found that I was drooling at the mouth at all the different sensations that had exploded inside began to radiate throughout the whole of my body. Nerves tingling, muscles spasmodically jerking, my pulses racing but all creating a sense of euphoria that flowed through me which was when I really then did relax.

Grandad must have felt this for his hands began to stroke the sides of my waist and upper thighs as he began to move himself back and forth as, for the first time, I was being fucked. Fucked by the man I loved, the fact that he was my grandfather had no meaning, for it was a rampant cock that was giving me the thrill of my life. The moving of his cock inside me, sliding back and forth in my canal, both soothing and exciting me at the same time. It was fucking great!

His hands holding my hips began to grip me tighter, his fingers digging in a little as he began to pull my hips back towards his forward thrusts. The action making my own erect cock to bounce up and down and my balls to swing beneath it. He was ramming himself into me and spittle was drooling out of my mouth at the way his cock was now ravaging my insides and fill me with such pleasure, pleasure that I had never felt before. He was grunting now at every inward push and I felt his cock really pulsate and jerk inside me and knew that he was shooting his load, if it was there, into the condom.

He leaned his weight onto my lower back and could hear him panting away, almost in time to the throbbing of his cock still inside me but not moving. But when it did, it began moving backwards and I knew that he was pulling out and my muscle began frantically trying to get a grip on the shaft as it moved and I gave out a cry as I felt it leaving me. That wonderful tool was leaving me! I tried to keep it there but lost the battle having a slight pain as the head left my ass and felt what seemed like cold air waft around my shrinking asshole.

I fell onto my side but was quickly up to turn round to see the smile on grandad's face and I knew I had tears in my eyes as I launched myself into his arms to kiss him with a passion that I didn't know I had inside me.

'Oh grandad! That was fucking great! It took me right over the bloody moon,' and rained kisses all over his face. Now having kissed him for the pleasure he had given me, I now wanted to pay homage to the object that had helped and fell down to pull off the condom, not bothering with tissues and took the head of his cock into my mouth and slobbered all over it, almost choking myself by trying to get the whole length of it inside to suck and chew. There wasn't any sperm to taste but that didn't matter as I sucked and kissed that wonder of nature that had just pleased me. It took an effort on his part to lift me off from my sucking of him and I then fell onto my back and just lay there looking at the man I loved. Relative or not as it was with me having been adopted, I loved him and knew that I would want to have him fuck me as much as he was able to.

'I love you grandad,' I said as he came into my arms for us to kiss

'I love you too Toby,' he said after our kisses.

'It…it won't turn me into being a homosexual would it?' I asked in a tremulous voice.

'I shouldn't think so,' he replied. 'Bi-sexual maybe. Though if you like it, then it's probable.'

'Bi-sexual?' I asked. Having heard the word but not quite sure of its real meaning.

'That you could swing two ways. Loving sex with a man as well as with a female. Though the difference is that you can only fuck a female for she can't fuck you, in the sexual acts I mean, whereas with a male, you can both fuck and be fucked. That would then show if you were bi-sexual or not,' he said. 'You like fucking me so now the question is, did you like being fucked by me?'

'Yes grandad, I did and can't wait for you to fuck me again,' I replied, loving the big smile I got from him which I'm sure I mirrored. 'It was so fantastic! I'm now ready to try and give you the same thrill that you have just given me.'

'I can feel that you are,' he replied with another grin, moving his body slightly on mine to move my cock a little that was being squashed between our bodies.

So for the second time that day, I fucked grandad, and now knowing the thrill he was getting by having my cock up inside him, made it even better for me and even crooned as I fucked him. I even got to fuck him twice after dinner before we both fell asleep exhausted.

CHAPTER VI

The next day he took me down to the port and one of the beaches there and had my first swim in the Mediterranean. It was lovely, the only drawback was having to wear my swimsuit for other people with small children were on the beach too. He only let me stay out in the sun for an hour as we didn't have the sun blocking cream with us. We had a tapas lunch at one of the many small restaurants there and we shared a bottle of wine between us. The downside to the day was that he couldn't raise himself up enough to let me have his cock inside me again though I was able to fuck him twice that night in bed.

Over the next two weeks, he took me all over the port and town with a visit to the big guns set up on top of a mountain. They had been built before the beginning of the Second World War to protect the bay with Spain remaining neutral throughout it. I took quite a few pictures of them and had me in quite a few standing beside these massive guns.

I loved the excursion we made the following week. It was to a nudist beach! I didn't think that they had them there in Spain. It was great to be able to strip off and swim naked in the sea. We had taken a Kool-box with us having our lunch inside as well as bottles of water. My body was now a lovely golden brown and didn't look out of place at seeing at least another twenty men naked too. Most of them were couples lying out in the sun on their towels. I even pointed out to grandad that I could see two of the couples were having oral sex and it turned me on to see this being done out in the open.

I begged grandad to see to me as my own erection was paining me, notwithstanding that he had an erection too. So there, out on the beach in the open air and under the bright sun, we went into the sixty nine position and sucked each other while playing with our balls until we both had our emissions to savour in our mouths before swallowing.

An hour later, he even let me fuck him as other men watched us and it wasn't long before I saw several other backsides up in the air and being fucked by their partner. As we hadn't taken any condoms with us, I had to go and wash myself in the sea as I had fucked him bare back, which I might add, preferred it to having to wear a rubber.

It was a terrific day out for me! The bonus being that he was able to rise up long enough to fuck me and give me the same thrill as he had done so before. This time him going bare back and I even cried out as I actually felt his sperm hit the insides of my canal. I was over the moon and in love with my grandad.

The whole holiday being a fuck fest with me having him several times a day with him now loving having me up inside him as much as I loved him fucking me when he was able to. He wasn't so keen when I fucked him while he was lying on his back with his legs in the air for he said that this position hurt his back so most of the time it was in the doggie fashion. The only other times with him on his back was when he laid out on the coffee table in the lounge which was just at the right height with me on my knees to fuck him. The other place for him to be on his back was the dining table where I was then standing upright, like my cock, as I had his legs up on my shoulders as I fucked him.

One other place we fucked was with me sitting on one of the hard backed chairs with my rampant cock held upright for him to straddle my thighs and slowly sink down onto my cock till he was sitting on my thighs. This way would could hold each other and kiss as he slowly moved himself up and down on me till I came inside him. Now that was a lovely one. He actually came himself once in this position, what with having his cock being squashed between us and technically masturbated as we moved and had his semen squish out and make a mess of our chests. Mind you, we had fun in licking it off of each other.

=oOo=

But tempus fugit and my holiday was almost over. It was nearly time for me to return to England to go back to college. After a lovely session of us both fucking each other, I laid in his arms and cried.

'Grandad. I don't want to go home,' tears running down my face. 'I love you and want to stay with you.' Through my tears, I could see that he also was crying as he held me tight to his chest.

'I would like you to stay Toby,' he managed to choke out, 'for I love you too, but you must finish your time at college, getting your degree and also be with your mother.'

So over those last two days I managed to fuck him a total of sixteen times and he was able to fuck me twice, both of us having to go bareback because we ran out of condoms. He said that he just loved feeling my sperm coat his insides as I came and I admit that I loved it too when I felt his. We both cried that last morning where I was able to raise myself up to fuck him twice, tears running down my face and onto his back. We never even stopped for breakfast such was our need for each other's rampant cock to give and receive the pleasure of the joining of our bodies together in this fashion. I was still crying when I asked if I could come out again during the next summer holidays to which he said I could as he would miss me when I'd gone.

I was slow packing my suitcase in the upstairs bedroom, only having slept in it the once, and eventually dragged it downstairs and said goodbye to Tom, giving the dog a big hug before following grandad out of the house so that he could lock up. We got in the car and had a quiet journey to the airport. There was not a lot I could say, sniffing back my tears at having to leave him. On arrival there, he carried my case to the check in point where I gave over the case to be weighed and sent off with its label and got my boarding clearance.

Just before passport control we went into a bear hug and both of us had tears in our eyes as we tried to say our goodbyes, our words being rather incoherent.

'Give this to your mother,' he said, passing an envelope to me. 'It's money for the fares for you and your mother to come out and spend Christmas with me.' This made me cry again as we had our last hugs.

'Thanks grandad. Thanks for having me,' I said, and gave out a funny giggle at realising what I had said.

'And you for having me,' he said with a sad smile on his face. 'Give my love to your mother and say that I will be looking forward to seeing you both at Christmas.'

'I'll tell her that I've had a wonderful time out here,' I said.

'Not everything!' He exclaimed, and gave out a laugh. 'She'd kill the both of us with what we've done together.'

'I won't but I will cherish what we did do grandad,' I said. And with a last pressing of cheeks together the way the Spanish do instead of a mouth to mouth kiss and quickly, almost ran through the control and only turned at the last minute to give him a wave before going into the waiting lounge.

I sat by myself for that hour or so, waiting for the plane and gently cried, missing him already, my mind going back over the fun and sex we had had over the past five and a half weeks. I heard the tannoy calling out my flight and sadly said goodbye to Spain as I went off to board the plane to take me back to England.

=oOo=

I don't remember much of the flight home I was so miserable but I perked up a little bit at being met at the airport by mum who gave me a big hug.

'My, how brown you look,' she exclaimed, holding me at arm's length. 'You must have enjoyed the sun being out there. And how was your grandad?'

'He was great!' I said. 'He couldn't have made me more welcome and here,' and I gave her the envelope. 'He wants us to go out there for Christmas with him.'

'How nice of him,' she replied, taking the envelope.

'How did New York go?' I asked, changing the subject.

'Fantastic! It couldn't have been better,' and she went on to tell all that she did and of the orders she got for her dresses. This took up the time for us to get home. Home now meant going back to college and for me, it was a miserable time in not being with grandad.

On my arrival back at college, the first thing I did was to write a letter to grandad to thank him again for having me with him and Spain and that I was looking forward to Christmas. There was only other thing that made college not so bad was when I got to fuck George. That was on the day of my nineteenth birthday which I played down as only one other boy knew.

He was a roommate of mine and we had often jerked each other off and one night when we were in his bed to do the same again was when I said that I would like to fuck him with what he was holding. My cock was rampant and really throbbing away. His answer was that I could if I sucked on him first.

This I did having learnt from grandad just how to do this and give the most satisfaction in doing so, taking George over the moon the way I did and pleased him immensely that I also swallowed his sperm, that being much more than grandad was able to produce. I was then able to fuck him and he said afterwards that he had liked it and wouldn't say no to more of the same thing if he could do the same to me next time.

So I didn't go without sex for the rest of the term, but still hankered after that cock of grandad for it was bigger and better in the way that he used it inside me as opposed to George.

When I had returned to college, I had entered the open university, using the laptop computer I had and began taking Spanish lessons and was doing quite well considering that when I started the only Spanish word I knew was gracias, thank you. When the month of December arrived, I began counting the days and that period of time seemed to take ages before we finally broke up for the Christmas break and found that mum had already booked the flights and so with our things packed, left for Spain and grandad.

Mum was as excited as I was when we finally were on the aircraft for takeoff, though for different reasons. Hers being that she hadn't seen him for nearly four years and me, well you know my reason.

He was there to greet us and I simply flew into his arms for a hug and the Gaelic kissing on the cheeks and saw the twinkle in his eyes as we did so and had to let go for him to greet mum. She was pleased as Punch to be with him again and she didn't stop talking the whole way from the airport to his home.

Mum remarked that the house needed a lick of paint and he agreed but said that he was getting too old to be climbing ladders but would see to it later. As it turned out, I actually did the painting a couple of years later, but did not know of this at the time. Tom, the dog went ballistic at seeing us, for he not only knew me but had remembered mum when she was last here. We eventually got into the house despite the cavorting and jumping around of Tom, and dumped our suitcases in the lounge.

'It's lovely to be back here with you dad,' she said to grandad. 'And how lovely you have decorated the room.' She was referring to the lounge where a Christmas tree was highly decorated with baubles and lights as well as the room having decorations all 'round the walls and hanging over some of the pictures.

'It wouldn't be Christmas without the tree and company,' he said with a smile accepting her kiss.

'Okay. I'll have the upstairs room and Toby can have the other downstairs one,' she said.

'Oh, er, well, there's been a slight change since you were here last Julie,' he said. 'I've gone and changed the other bedroom down here into a sort of office and library. Come and see.' He took her hand and led her to what had once been a bedroom.

'Oh. Where's Toby going to sleep?' she asked. That's where I jumped in.

'I don't mind bunking with granddad, mum,' I said. 'That is if grandad doesn't mind. He's got a double bed in there.'

'Well, if you don't mind having the tyke in there with you,' mum said, and I felt my cock start to make itself known at what will happen with me sleeping with grandad again. She then picked up her suitcase and took it upstairs and when she was out of sight, I flew into grandad's arms and kissed him.

'It's so good to be back with you again,' I gushed, letting him feel the erection I had inside my trousers. 'And to be sleeping with you too,' and kissed him again.

'Be careful Toby,' he said in a low voice. 'Only in bed can we really speak our minds.' With this admonishment, understood and agreed.

'Don't worry. I'll keep mum.' The English slang word for not speaking out of that that shouldn't be spoken.

It wasn't long before mum came back downstairs. 'Can I do dinner?' she asked of grandad. 'We haven't eaten since breakfast and that was quite early this morning.'

'By all means,' he replied, pouring out two drinks for him and mum who had already gone into the kitchen.

Grandad, bless him, pointed to the bottle he had put down as he took the two glasses into the kitchen letting me pour out one for myself. Now mum is a bloody good cook and it wasn't long before there was a lovely smell coming from the kitchen and I did my part by laying the table for us to enjoy the lovely casserole she had cooked.

After that grand meal, we sat in the lounge in front of the log burning fire while she told grandad of her trip to the States and of the orders she had obtained in the doing so. Now mum can talk the hind legs off a donkey when she gets going and I saw that it was close on ten o'clock when I gave out a big yawn and said that I was tired and wanted to go to bed,

'You do that darling,' mum said to me.

'Er, grandad. What side of the bed do you sleep on?' I asked, knowing damn well which side it was, but it was for the benefit of mum that I asked the question and saw the smile that he hid in my asking the question.

'I usually sleep in the middle, but as we are having to share it, I'll be on the side closest to the window if you don't mind.' I gave him a smile back that mum couldn't see.

'Okay,' and I got up and gave mum a kiss on the cheek and gave one to grandad. 'Goodnight then,' I said and went off and quickly undressed and got into the bed where I had had quite a lot of fun in the last time I was in it.

It could have only been twenty minutes before I heard grandad plead tiredness, though it seemed that much longer to me, lying there naked in his bed with a massive hard on that I didn't dare touch in case I shot my load before letting him have it.

I heard them say their goodnights and saw the lounge light go out and he was there in the room with me and I watched as he undressed to be as naked as I was, his penis at half-mast as he got into bed beside me. With it being winter time, we had a duvet cover instead of the single sheet that we had used during the summer.

As soon as he was in the bed, I rolled over on top of him, squashing my erection between our stomachs as I kissed him. I also felt that he had become somewhat aroused too at the thought of him fucking me as I had the same in wanting to fuck him.

'I love you grandad and I want to thank you for letting us come for Christmas,' and had to stifle my giggles at using the word come. 'I've been wanting to cum for some time now, and the place for me to cum is inside you,' I breathed into his ear.

'And I want to cum inside of you too,' he panted.

'I've been counting not only the days, but the weeks to be back here with you. In this bed, for us to make love together, and now here we are and I can feel that you want me as much as I want you,' I said as I kissed him.

'I've been counting the days too Toby. I really did miss you when you left and it was only the knowing that you would be back here at this time that kept me going. 'I missed having you here in this bed with me, and feeling your hard cock as it is now, begging to be used inside me. Fuck me Toby! Fuck my brains out.'

'Oh grandad, you don't know how much I have wanted to do as you ask. I only hope that you will stay as hard as I can feel now, to be able to do the same to me. But let me fuck you first so that you will be that much harder to be able to do the same to me and fuck my brains out too.'

'Oh Toby, I do love you so,' he whispered into my ear.

'I think I love you the same,' I said as I kissed him and rolled off for him to get into position. 'Do you have more condoms in the drawer' I asked.

'Bugger the condoms,' he said getting up onto his knees. 'Just fuck me you randy little sod. Let me feel you coming inside me.'

'What about the cream?' I asked as I got onto the bed.

'Fuck the cream, just bugger me!' he said, saying this as though it was through gritted teeth.

So I got between his legs and put the head of my cock to his ring piece and began to push myself into him. Boy, he wasn't relaxing, or was it the lack of not having any cream there that was stopping me from entering him. I was pushing quite hard but not getting in and so took a leaf from his book and gave the cheek of his bum a hefty slap and voila, the head of my cock slipped in.

He gave out a big gasp. 'Christ! Did you have to do that,' he said.

'Well you didn't want the cream and I couldn't get in,' I said, knowing I had a smirk on my face, but I was there, only the head I know, but I could feel the heat and I'm sure he could feel it throbbing as his muscle began to flex itself round the head. 'Now just relax and enjoy it.'

'You bugger,' he panted and I'm sure that it was said with a smile as I began to once again fuck my grandad.

And it was lovely to again be behind him, moving my cock back and forth in his tight canal, enjoying the feel of him reacting to the internal massage he was getting and giving me another thrill in the fucking of him. He gave out some lovely sighs as I moved and wished it could last longer than I knew it would for I could feel that I wasn't far off cumming.

He knew this too as I began to move a little faster and with more forcing of my hips up to the cheeks of his bum, feeling my balls smacking them at the forward thrusts. Also by my gripping his hips tighter as I came to my peak and held my body up tight to his as my hips began to jerk as I came inside him, giving him that life giving seed that was doomed by not finding an egg to fertilise.

'Oh Toby,' he gasped. 'I can really feel it hitting my insides you darling boy.' Which was music to my ears as my hips kept jerking away sending shot after shot of my sperm into his rectum until I had nothing left to give and finally came to a stop, panting quite heavily as I leaned over his back.

'I love doing this grandad,' I managed to get out in between taking deeps breaths, 'and hope that you are fit enough to see to me in the same way.'

'Toby, as much as I love where you are now and hate the part of you pulling out, don't leave it too long for I have got a lovely big hard on with the thrill you have just given me.'

He gave out a cough when he'd finished speaking and I felt the whole of his insides contract quite strongly round my cock as he did so. But with me now wanting him to fuck me, straightened up and pulled out to his cries of dismay at losing what had just given him his pleasure. But I wanted him inside me, to use his erect cock to pleasure me before it deflated.

I wasn't going to waste time by washing myself at this moment, so when he rolled over onto his side, I was quickly down in the position and ready for him to get behind me and push his erection up inside me.

'I'm a coward grandad, so use some cream please,' I said as he moved behind me and leaned over my back and was just able to reach the cream pot.

I had felt his cock give my balls a poke as he did this and it gave me thoughts about later sucking on his balls which I know excited him as much as sucking on the head of his cock. I gave out a flinch as I felt the cold cream being coated at the entrance to my ass and waited and gave out a shiver as I felt the head position itself at the entrance to my grotto. The only time that my grotto held treasure was when his cock was in there and I gave out a grunt as I felt it being planted in there.

The pain was there again as he widened the orifice that quickly subsided as his shaft filled me and had his thighs up tight to my rear end, feeling it pulsate and throb as I caressed it with my sphincter muscle.

'I've been dreaming of this all the time since you were last inside me grandad,' I said, still feeling a slight twinge, but this was overridden by the thrill I felt at having him once more inside to give me pleasure and take me to heaven with the massaging of my inner being. 'It's as if I was really home again being here with you and having you fuck me,' I had carried on speaking as he smoothly slid back and forth inside me, setting all my nerves atingle and joy to my heart that it was my grandad who was making love to me in the only real way that we could make love to each other, apart from the sucking of our cocks.

I'm sure he lasted longer than me in his fucking, which I didn't object to as I simply loved what he was doing to please me, taking me to heaven in this act of anal sex. But I remembered a passage in one of his books that misery seems to last forever while joy passes in a flash. I think I quoted it right but it's true for he was soon ramming himself up tight to my rear and I actually felt his seed splash my insides as he came, pumping away enough to make me drool at having felt him cum inside of me and not into a condom.

I gave out that usual cry as I felt him pulling out of me, feeling bereft of that lovely fucking tool he had used inside me, falling forward and then finding it an effort to rise up and follow him into the bathroom where we both stood either side of the basin to wash our deflating and deflated cocks under the stream of warm water, me taking that bit longer by having to make sure that my foreskin was back far enough to ensure that it was really clean.

Grandad was back on the bed waiting for me and held his arms open for me to fall into and have him cuddle me.

'That was simply lovely grandad. I'm glad you were able to keep it up,' I said between kisses. 'You don't know how much I missed you. Not being able to sleep with you, having you suck on me and having to jerk myself off making believe that it was you holding my cock until I came onto my stomach, wishing that it had been your mouth.'

To try and prove how much I had missed him, went down under the duvet to take all of his cock into my mouth, my nose into his pubic hair to get the smell of him as I sucked and gently chewed on his soft rubbery cock until I had to surface for some fresh air. We kissed and cuddled some more until I fell asleep.

CHAPTER VII

'I've just had a lovely dream,' I said sleepily as I came awake, still lying in his arms, wondering if I had moved at all during the night. 'That I was here with it just being the two of us and we were making love. You were on your knees and I was behind you and you said that you loved me as I stuck my cock up inside you.'

'Well I do love you Toby, very much, and I can't think of anything better than you doing what you've just dreamed about.' So again without using a condom, I got up between his legs, him having assumed the position to be fucked in, though this time, I had no problem of moving myself up into the inside body heat of his for him to gasp and say how wonderful my cock was, especially being where it was then. I stroked his waist as I moved myself in and out of him until I reached my peak and gave him the contents of my balls to his small cries of pleasure at feeling every hit of my semen that coated his canal.

After I had pulled out, he fell over onto his back and pulled me down and kissed me. 'I think you love me as much as I love you grandad,' I said.

'That I do Toby, that I do,' he sighed. 'I wish we had got together earlier.'

'So do I,' I said before giving him one more kiss before getting out of bed to wash myself and see to the other things that one does in a bathroom.

Though we shared the shower in the washing of each other, taking longer than necessary over our now not so private parts. We were dressed when mum came down from the upstairs bedroom and began to cook breakfast, after which, we had to go shopping for mum said that grandad's cupboards were like those of Mother Hubbard by being nearly bare.

After lunch we sat in front of the log fire and watched a DVD, one of the few that mum had brought out with us till dinner time, where, after which, we watched another one. I was glad when it was over for I'd seen it before and then pleaded tiredness and kissed both mum and grandad before going to bed to wait for him, my lover to join me. I quivered at the thought of really saying that he was my lover for that really what he was in spite of him being my grandad, he was the man I loved and wished that I could stay with him for all the time to come.

It was nearly an hour before I heard mum and grandad saying goodnight to each other, me having an erection the whole time and not wanting to play with myself as I waited for grandad to come to bed to be with me and to let me use my erection and give us both the pleasure of sex between us.

'I thought she was never going to go to bed,' he whispered to me as he undressed and got into bed with me.

I was quickly onto my side, half laying my naked body on his, letting him feeling the erection that I had maintained for the past hour as I kissed him. That was before I moved down the bed and took his cock into my mouth and sucked on him and heavens above, he actually was able to cum for me to move it around in my mouth before swallowing it. I worked my way back up and into his arms for him to kiss me, in spite of me still having traces of his sperm on my tongue.

'You have a better cock to suck on than George,' I said.

'George? Who's George?' he asked, so I told him of what George and I did on the night of my birthday. He seemed a bit flummoxed at me having sex with another male. He went on to say that he hoped that I had worn a condom but didn't pick up the fact that I hadn't said yes or no, for in fact I had gone bare back when I had fucked him.

'So you sucked and fucked another male?' he finished up saying.

'Yes, but you've got a better and bigger cock than he had. You taste much better and I found that I prefer using my cock with you grandad,' I said as I hugged him. 'Do I have to use a condom with you?'

'Not if you don't want to for I haven't had anyone else fuck me and I love the feeling of you coming inside me. Only with me, wear one if you want me to suck on you afterwards,' he said.

'Okay,' I said, my cock beginning to hurt me such was my need for a fuck. 'No condom and you can suck on me after I've had a good wash.' I rolled off of him and waited for him to get up onto his knees and I put some cream on the head of my erection as he did so until he was ready with his legs apart for me to get in between them.

What bliss it was to once again be fucking my grandad, knowing that not only did he love me but loved me fucking him as much now as I loved him fucking me.

'As lovely as ever grandad,' I panted as I came to a stop, leaning over his rear end, my cock still throbbing away inside him and loving the feel of his muscle flexing itself round the shaft.

'You can say that again,' he panted beneath me.

'As lovely as ever grandad,' and gave out a giggle as I straightened up and began to pull out of him getting that little cry from him as I did so, feeling the air that seemed cold after the heat of his inner body.

'The only part I don't like when having sex like this with you,' he grunted, 'is when you are pulling out.' He slipped down onto his side as I got off the bed to go and wash myself and found him facing me when I returned to the bedroom. So I got on the bed and into his open arms for him to hold and cuddle me as we kissed.

'You're a fine figure of a man now. A bit more flesh on your bones and you'll have many a woman chasing after you,' he said giving me a squeeze.

'No men?' I giggled, loving his arms round me, wondering if it would be the same with another man holding me as he was now, feeling his cock pressing up against my still half erect one.

'Them too maybe, but don't become a slut by taking just anybody,' he said as he rolled me onto my back and began kissing his way down my body and taking me into his mouth when he got down that far. With it only being half way to being an erection, he was able to take the whole thing into his hot mouth and had his nose move about in my pubic hairs. He sucked and gently chewed away at me for a few minutes before releasing me and moving down a little more, pushing my cock up onto my lower stomach and surprised me by taking my balls into his mouth.

These he moved about as he sucked on them, first one then the other before moving both of them round in his mouth again. I couldn't help giving out a small groan at the pleasure he was giving me until he stopped, releasing them and coming back up the bed into my now open arms for me to kiss him.

'Gracias,' I said after that kiss.

'What's this? Speaking Spanish?' he cried in a low voice.

'I started taking Spanish lessons as soon as I got back to school,' I said. 'I'm even doing the Open University course in it.'

'Well keep it up,' he said. 'Your cock too, for I love it. Especially when it's up inside me, fucking me and you cumming and coating my insides with your semen.'

'I love doing it too grandad. You're so hot and tight inside. You're tighter than Scrooge, and I love it when your muscle plays with the shaft.'

'Oh I love you Toby,' he said. His voice muffled by having his face pressed in against my neck. 'I love you for being my grandson and the fun we have together.' This brought tears to my eyes.

'I love you too grandad,' lifting his head up to see that he had tears in his eyes too as I then kissed him. 'I love being with you and inside you and more so when you are inside me.'

We kept hugging each other as tears flowed down both our faces until he pulled himself out of my arms and moved back down the bed, kissing and nibbling at the nipples on my chest before carrying on down to suck and play with both my cock and balls until it was up hard again. This led to me fucking him again that night until I was exhausted and after washing myself for the second time, got back into bed and fell asleep with him stroking my body.

=oOo=

It's a good job that I had been so tired that morning and not having sex with grandad, for mum came into the bedroom with two cups of coffee to wake us both up. Grandad was lying on his side facing the window and I was on my side too, but close up to his back, she didn't make any comment of us being in this position but might have had said something if she had been able to see beneath the duvet, for I had a massive hard on and it was pressed right up against grandad's back. Well more between the crease of his bum to be precise.

Grandad, the bugger, on coming awake and feeling where my cock was, moved about as though getting more comfortable as mum put his coffee down on the bedside cabinet top. He had moved so that my erection slipped down between his legs which he brought together, trapping my cock between them and kept moving as if he was masturbating me as he thanked mum for the coffee. I had to bury my head in the pillow for I'm sure that it had gone red with him doing what he was with my cock.

In fact, I actually came while she was still in the room, feeling it shoot out over his legs and sheets and had to stifle the groan in the pillow as I did so. It was only when she left the bedroom did I put my hand down over his thigh to find that he was up and hard. I then dived down under the duvet as he rolled over onto his back for me to take him into my mouth and sucked on him and made him come in my mouth. There wasn't a lot of sperm but enough for me to move around in my mouth before swallowing it.

After giving the head of his cock a kiss, I moved up and out from under the duvet and gave a quick look at the doorway before giving grandad a kiss. 'What a way to wake up grandad with mum in the room too,' I laughed. He did as well as he got out of bed and moved round and pulled me out and pushed me ahead of him into the bathroom into where the shower was.

'Your face is covered in semen the same as my legs,' he said as he turned on the shower.

'I didn't know we had any navy men here,' I laughed and had the water spray directed straight at my face, him laughing at the pun of semen and seamen.

Washed clean, we soon got dressed and went and had breakfast that mum cooked and with it being the day before Christmas Eve, went shopping later. We picked up the turkey that grandad had already ordered and went into other shops, where in one of them I tried out my Spanish.

'Pueda tengo un kilo de fresas,' I asked of the girl behind the counter and got a smile as she got what I asked for, pleased that she understood me.

'What's that you said Toby?' grandad asked me in a surprised voice.

'A kilo of strawberries grandad. I know that you've got a bottle of champagne in the fridge and I read somewhere that strawberries tasted better when dipped in champagne,' I said giving him a sweet smile and saw the glint in his eyes as he knew that I was quoting from one of the books he had written. Even mum was impressed with me speaking in Spanish but didn't know of the connection that I had said to grandad.

'He's getting rather good in his Spanish,' she said and that was it with the shopping. We stopped off at a café and had some tapas for lunch and back home later, grandad had to smile as I dipped some strawberries into his glass of champagne and let him see me sucking on them before eating them. I think it goes without saying that I fucked him twice that night before going to sleep after a kiss and cuddle.

=oOo=

We lazed away on Christmas Eve watching the television both of us helping mum do the meals and then going to bed where grandad and I had a lovely sex session between us before falling asleep.

Mum was up early in the morning to put the turkey in the oven so grandad and I had to forgo any sex with her being up and about. We then opened up the presents we had bought each other that had been kept under the Christmas tree. Lunch was brilliant and we made pigs of ourselves before sitting in front of the log fire to hear the Queen's Christmas speech to the nation.

After which, we played cards and only picked at food things later instead of having dinner until I gave out a yawn and said that I was tired and so with giving them both a kiss, went to bed to wait for grandad to join me. And join we did after we knew that mum had gone to bed too.

I had managed to get grandad up and hard by sucking on his cock and playing with his balls until he was ready to fuck me.

'This is the best Christmas present you are giving me grandad,' I said as he moved his hard cock back and forth inside of me and gave out a little cry of joy when he came and me feeling his sperm hit my inside channel.

Though I didn't like the removal of his lovely cock from my ass when he had finished in his fucking of me. I was then fully rampant and let him see it after he came back from the bathroom after washing himself. I was going to fuck him bare back as well for we'd run out of condoms again and it wasn't something that he could buy with mum in attendance while we had shopped for food.

He also loved it when I fucked him, just as much as I did and got a wonderful hug and kiss after I had washed myself. We lay there kissing and stroking each other and in the joy of fucking him and being fucked, forgot about the other Christmas present that I had bought him. One that I had kept hidden from mum when I packed my own suitcase. I had put it under the bed and I now rolled over and got it out and gave it to him.

'I got this extra present for you,' I said and watched to see his face when he unwrapped it and found that it was a rubber dildo. A replica of a circumcised cock with batteries in the base. 'It's for you to use when we've gone and you can think of it as being me every time you use it.' He had a laugh when he had seen it and gave me a big kiss and I wanted him to try it for size, saying this with a laugh

'Would you like to try it while you suck on me and then think that I'm in two places at the same time?' I asked with a giggle and he had to laugh again and agreed. So I got the cream pot out and put some onto the head of the dildo and got behind him as he went up onto his knees.

'Be slow and gentle with it,' he said as I put it to his ring piece and slowly began to push this fake cock up into his backside.

He gave out some grunts until I had it all the way in his ass before turning it on. I quickly then got round on the bed and slithered my body down on my back with my legs astride of his so that I could bring my groin to be under his lowering head. He lifted up my rampant throbbing cock and took me into his mouth to start sucking on me as the dildo vibrated up in his backside.

He was gurgling as he sucked and teased the head of my cock and to try to bring me up to an orgasm without using his hands, for if he had of tried, he would have fallen over. But he didn't need to use one as just his hot mouth and the way he used his tongue soon brought me up to my peak and began to buck my hips up towards him.

He didn't lose one drop as I began shooting my semen into his mouth, hoping that he was getting pleasure at the other end at the same time, which he did as he told me later. Though he would rather it had been me behind him for he missed having me come inside giving him, as he put it, the icing on the cake, though rather up inside his canal.

CHAPTER VIII

The New Year arrived with us having some drinks to celebrate this, me declining more than two glasses of champagne and we only stayed up to see the celebrations in London on the television, though it was an hour later than that of Spain, and with that over, went to bed where I was able to thank grandad again for having us with him and having me up inside him for the first time of the New Year. Unfortunately for me, he couldn't respond with the amount that he had drunk that evening.

But he did on our last night, just loving his big cock moving inside me and feeling him come inside me, not a lot, but enough to give me the same pleasure that I gave him afterwards.

It was a sombre morning for both grandad and myself though mum was looking forward to getting her designs made up to be able to fulfil the order for the States. Me, downcast at leaving grandad and him at not having me in his bed at night. There were tears in our eyes as we kissed him goodbye at the airport and before we knew it, mum and I were back in London, and into the cold.

The only thing I had to look forward to was that grandad had agreed, with mum's consent, that I could spend the next summer's holiday with him once again. I did miss him when I was all alone in my bed that night and actually cried that he wasn't there with me, to hold and kiss me either before or after our sexual couplings. I even cried that first night back at college but gave myself a mental slap and to get control of myself. It's only for six months and you'll be back with grandad.

So I knuckled down to my studies, bringing Spanish up to the fore and because of the time I spent in these lessons, got an excellent pass mark from the Open University on my Spanish language. I even got to fuck George again and had him fuck me, though it wasn't the same as being with grandad. It was after my session with George that brought back home to me just how much I loved grandad and it was then that I made the decision as to what I was going to do in the future. That is something that we will come to in time, but as the summer holidays got closer, the more agitated I became and was glad when the final day of college came before breaking up for the summer holiday.

Mum knew that I loved my grandad, but not knowing just how far that we did love each other, so she assumed that with my hasty packing of my suitcase was to be back out in the sunshine in Spain more than my wanting to be back in bed and making love with him. She came with me to the airport and kissed me goodbye, telling me to behave myself again, like she did the last time with me telling her that grandad and myself got on well together and that she had nothing to worry about. He had been told when and at what time I would be arriving in Spain and he was there to greet me.

How my heart raced when I came out of the collection of baggage area and saw him waiting for me. I flew into his arms for that lovely big hug though we only kissed in the Gaelic fashion with the pressing of our cheeks together though it was on the lips when we got into his car. I was over the moon to be back with him and had an erection for the whole of the hour's journey to his home. I couldn't help but keep blabbering on as he did about how happy we both were with me being back in Spain with him. I didn't have to remark on how hot it was compared to England this time for he already knew this.

We eventually arrived and I got a lovely welcome greeting from Tom, jumping up all over me, licking my face as much as he could until he was told to behave himself and let me get into the house properly.

'It's great to be back here with you grandad,' I said. 'I've missed you so much.'

'I've missed you too,' he said, and I could see that he fighting back the tears as we went into a hug and kissed each other.

'Can we go straight to bed? I've been dreaming of this for weeks now and I do really need you.' Feeling the tears in my eyes too as we held and looked at each other, both of us wanting the same for I could feel that he had an erection the same as I had.

'I can't think of anything better,' he replied and we went straight off into the bedroom where we undressed as quick as we could, both of us showing the erections we had and saw the way they bounced about as we got onto his bed.

'Oh grandad I want you,' I gasped in our clinch, our cocks getting squashed between our naked bodies.

'I want you too,' he said, his voice full of emotion as he pulled himself away from me to turn round on the bed to show his backside to the world as he assumed the position that he was happy to be fucked in. I moved too, to get between his open legs and had the thrill run through me that I was once again to be going in the right direction by guiding my cock to the entrance of his backside. My hands then up on his hips, neither of us bothering about using either cream or condom as I leaned into him and had the joy of my erect cock moving back into that tight orifice of his ass.

He gave out some grunts at the speed and pressure at which I penetrated him and I was back in heaven at feeling the heat of his body and the tightness of his canal as my cock smoothly slid up inside him. It was bliss beyond words and my whole body was suffused with euphoria as my cock pulsated inside him and had his muscle there flexing away at my shaft as I savoured this six month long dream of being where I was with my grandad.

I ploughed his meadow with my tool that seemed to have been made for this specific purpose of giving him the pleasure of being ploughed and me for having the right tool to do so. I couldn't help but croon as I moved myself back and forth inside that heated canal, loving the experience that once found, needed repeating time after time. I loved grandad and never more so that when I was behind and fucking him, drooling at the thought that within another few minutes he would be pleasuring me in the same fashion.

I hadn't masturbated for two days and so I had, well it seemed to me, twice as much sperm inside my balls which I was now about to spray into his hot and tight canal. Boy, did I cum or not. It didn't seem to end, holding his hips in a firm grasp as my hips did the pumping and my balls reacting to these forward thrusts, sending out the seed that would never take root. But the thrill and exhilaration there was then in this act of having sex with another male in this fashion taking me to heights that had seemed impossible, but I was at the peak and cried out with joy at the reaching of it.

'Yes!' I cried out as I cummed for the first time, really pulling him back onto me with that hard first thrust.

'Yes!' cried out grandad as he felt it hit the sides of his tight canal. There were just grunts after that he emitted as I gave him several more shots as I humped him, finally coming to a halt, leaning over his back and breathing heavily.

'I really needed that grandad,' I panted as I pulled out of him. He fell onto his side and looked at my still hard and steaming cock.

'I needed you too,' he said. 'Go and wash yourself and then let me fuck you.'

I could see that he was still up hard and knew that I wanted him to fuck me with it, and so I was quickly off the bed and went and washed before returning to find him sitting on his heels near the end of the bed, his cock still upright and waiting to be used. I got on the bed and stayed on my knees as I turned and leaned forward onto my forearms, bending my back downwards to lift my backside high up in the air. I felt the bed moving as he shuffled forward and had his hands come and hold my hips as the head of his erection unerring found the entrance to my cave and gave out that flinch at the first touch. I felt the pressure of the head begin to widen me and he suddenly spoke that nearly made me laugh.

'Open Sesame!' was the words and I should have called him Aladdin, for I suddenly relaxed and had the head of his cock enter me. Oh what joy it was to feel it throb and pulsate as his cock slid easily into my backside, filling me with happiness too as his hips came up to the cheeks of my bum. Now came the soothing massage as his cock easily slid back and forth, defeating the encircling grip my muscle was giving to the shaft of his cock. Nerves became excited and tremors ran through my body and tingles ran up and down my spine as he ploughed into me and he lasted nearly twice as long as I had in his shafting of me. I'm sure I felt his emission, albeit a small one, an aid to the smooth moving of him inside me until he came to a full stop. Me gasping, him panting and his cock still throbbing at the pleasure that he had given to both of us.

'It feels bigger than ever grandad,' I said between pants and gave out that cry as I had that wonderful fucking tool being pulled out of me, feeling the cold air waft round my shrinking ring piece. I turned round on the bed but he stopped me from going down on him.

'Let me wash it first,' he said, pushing me to one side so that he could get off the bed. I moved back on the bed and watched him through the door washing himself and after he had dried himself, came back to where I had my arms open and he came in between them for us to kiss and hold each other in the joy of us both being back together again, to kiss, to fuck and to love one another as we had done before.

'I love you to bits grandad,' I said between kisses.

'I love you too Toby. It's grand to have you back here with me, more so when we are in this bed again,' he said, his eyes shining and I could see the love in them and hoped that mine mirrored his for I loved him more now than my mother.

'I've missed being here too grandad and its grand to be back having missed you so much,' I said before giving him a really passionate kiss. This was returned and we stayed kissing and stroking each other for a little while before I broke free from our cuddling and moved down the bed to take his soft flaccid penis into my mouth to suck and gently chew on. I had turned round in moving down and he now had taken my rather limp cock into his mouth and felt him push the foreskin down and gave out a groan as his tongue moved over and round my G string.

It wasn't long before he had made my cock rise up to being a full erection and it wasn't long before I released his cock that was still soft so to speak and tell him that I wasn't far off cumming.

'Let it go,' he mumbled round the head of my cock which was all he had in his mouth now, and so I let go. Moving my hips towards his face as I sent my seed deep into his throat with the first of six emissions. I felt the extra suction as he swallowed what I had given him and had his tongue now rove over the head as it was exposed to the cool air of the bedroom. With me now being out of his mouth, let go of his and turned round on the bed and moved up to get back into his arms.

'Lovely as ever Toby,' he said between kisses. 'Now let's have a shower and get something to eat, you must be hungry.'

'I was for you grandad but now it's for my stomach,' I said, and let go of him and we then left the bed and went and had our shower where we both washed each other, another pleasure that we seemed to have in the doing of this. 'We should shave your balls grandad,' I said as my hand was moving them about as I washed them. 'I kept getting bits of your hair stuck in between my teeth last time.'

'We can do that after we've eaten. I've tried doing it myself before but gave up after having nicked myself a couple of times,' he said. So after drying ourselves, we put on sarongs and went and prepared our evening meal and I showed him how much my cooking had improved.

'Well it smells good enough to eat,' grandad said, and it was and he praised me as well as saying we would have to go shopping the next day to get more food in as it was market day in the town.

'Oh good. I've been doing very well in learning my Spanish,' telling him how I got my pass marks in the language. 'I can really try out what I've learned while at the market. I've brought my Spanish book with me but I think they will understand me. Though the books I want to read are those that you've written.'

'Well I'm afraid that I haven't written anything new since you've been gone. I haven't been able to concentrate enough, but there's still quite a lot that you haven't read yet.'

With dinner over and the things used, washed up and put away, I was anxious to get hold of his balls and shave them clean of the hairs that they had.

'Where's the best place for us to do this, the shaving of your balls?' I asked.

'I suppose the bed would be best. It's as good a place as anywhere else,' he replied, and so off back to the bedroom we went. He brought a small bowl out from the kitchen with him and this I half filled with warm water from the bathroom while he laid a towel out on the bed. He'd also taken in the shaving cream, razor and a flannel and with his sarong off, lay on his back on the bed, the towel now being below his open legs as I put the bowl next to him and got on the bed between his legs and sprayed some foam over his balls, keeping his flaccid cock out of the way.

'Take it nice and easy so you don't cut me,' he said, using his hand to keep his dick out of the way.

'I will grandad,' I said, working the foam round his balls which I then stretched out to make the sac as tight and as smooth as I could. Then with my left hand holding him in a tight grip, used my right hand with the razor to begin shaving his balls. I was very gentle and careful as I drew the razor down with each stroke, only doing a couple before rinsing off the cream with the flannel to check that I was doing it right. Then a little more foam to do some more until I finally sat back quite pleased with myself now looking at his hairless balls in their bag.

'We can also trim the pubic hairs,' I said, getting off the bed to get the scissors from the bathroom and then teased him by having them just above his cock as I kept opening and closing the blades.

'Don't cut that,' grandad said. 'I still need it to piss through.'

'And to put it up inside me when it's ready, so I'm not likely to shorten it,' I said with a laugh as I began to act the barber in trimming all the hair round his cock until he had a very light bush there. I then gave the whole area another wash and dried him and sat up and saw that I had done a bloody good job and couldn't resist the urge to now suck on his hairless balls. This made him give out a gasp and me the pleasure (as well as him), of having them in my mouth to suck and move about without getting hairs stuck in between my teeth again.

'Lovely,' I said when I let go of him and straightened up and showed him my teeth which I rubbed with a finger. 'Look. No hairs,' and grinned at him and put the foam, razor and bowl onto the floor and then fell on top of him to kiss him on the lips for a few minutes before moving down to kiss and nip at his nipples. I now had a nice erection so carried on kissing his body as I moved down the bed. His legs had opened for me to get in between them and took his still flaccid cock in my mouth but gave up after a few minutes as I couldn't raise it up.

So I let go of that and put my hands under his legs and lifted them up so that they rested on my shoulders. This action brought his backside up off the bed a little way and with me straightening up was able to get the head of my cock to the entrance of his ass hole. I looked down at his face to see that he had a big grin there though it turned to a slight grimace as I pushed my hips forward and had my cock enter him. I leaned my body forward so that I could support myself with both arms rigid down by his sides, his legs being kept up by my arms as I began to fuck him in this position. I was lovely to be able to move and fuck him and see him smile up at me as I did so.

I saw the sparks in his eyes as he felt my first emission coat his inside canal and his lips puckered in a kiss as more was sent up into him. With me thus being drained, suddenly felt weak and collapsed on top of him, his legs sliding off my arms but I was still able to keep my hard cock up inside of him as our chests came together. My sweaty body that been dripping sweat onto his stomach earlier, was now smearing it across his chest. With me being almost six foot tall now, I was able to stay in there and yet still kiss him, his arms coming round onto my sweaty back to hold me tight, his muscle flexing round my still throbbing cock buried inside of him.

'Wonderful Toby, just wonderful,' he gasped between kisses.

'So are you grandad,' I panted and could feel that us having fucked in this position had aroused him for it felt quite hard squashed between us. I don't know where he got the strength from for he was able to then roll us both over so that I was now on my back with him on top of me.

My cock had now slipped out of him with this action and now felt his cock moving to slip down between the cheeks of my bum. Somehow, I managed to wriggle my legs free and lifted them up and got them up onto his shoulders and felt his erection touch my rosebud. Grandad didn't need telling what to do and had him enter and fill me with his hard cock.

'Fucking lovely grandad,' I gasped as he filled me with not only his cock but pleasure too. He smiled back down at me and I loved this grandad of mine more than life itself as he fucked me, taking me to heaven and back as he had his dry orgasm, not actually cumming inside of me but having the same experience as if he was ejaculating. He came to a faltering stop and so eased himself on top of me, keeping himself inside me until he was able to kiss me. I could feel the beating of his heart as he lay on top of me, still moving himself slowly inside me.

'I really, really love you grandad,' I sighed, flexing my muscle round his cock as he finally came to a stop.

'I love to too Toby,' he said and I could see tears in his eyes that he tried to hold back but was unable to stop them from slowly beginning to roll down his cheeks. I held him tight to me, now starting to cry myself.

'I wish I could stay here forever with you grandad,' as I held him even tighter to me as I felt him slowly start to slip out of me.

We eventually separated to lay on our sides facing each other, stroking each other's body, feeling his hand linger on my bum the longest and having the odd kiss which we both seemed to welcome in our love for each other and I could feel tiredness creeping through me.

'Grandad?'

'Yes?' his voice sounding sleepy like mine.

'Can I take Tom out for a run with me in the morning? I've been going out every morning to get the exercise since Christmas,' I said.

'By all means. He needs the exercise too for he's getting to be fat like me,' he replied.

'You're not fat grandad, just built big,' I managed to say before falling asleep.

CHAPTER IX

I was awake before grandad and so I slid down the bed and began to suck on his morning erection, which though not as hard as it could be, it was enough for me to have in my mouth to enjoy waking him up in this fashion. His body reacted as though he could cum in my mouth but it was just another dry orgasm and when his body relaxed under me, knew and felt his cock start to wilt and so with giving the head of his cock a kiss, moved back up the bed.

'Good morning grandad,' I said, grinning at his sleepy look. 'And it's a lovely morning too!'

'God,' he groaned. 'You're bloody cheerful.'

'Yes, for I've just sucked on the cock of the man that I love. You didn't cum though,' I frowned.

'You had it all last night. It takes me longer now that I'm getting old and not as young as you,' he said, stroking my back and feeling my erection pressing up against his thigh.

'You're as young as the person you feel,' I laughed, remembering that I had heard this said by someone whose name I couldn't recall. 'So how do you feel now?'

'With both hands as usual,' he laughed, coming out with that old joke. 'Now that I'm awake. Let me feel that what is pressing hard up against my side,' and he pushed me off of him and reached down and took hold of my throbbing cock.

Grandad moved slowly down the bed, kissing my chest, my stomach and then the head of my erection as he opened his mouth and his tongue moved over his lips before they went round the foreskin and pushed it down to bare the flesh to his tongue. It was like a small electric shock that ran up from the head all through my body and made my cock twitch in his mouth. I couldn't help the groan at the pleasure he began to give me as he sucked and gently moved his teeth round the base of the head.

His hand was moving the skin of my cock up and down, gently at first, sliding over the solid flesh beneath it, steadily gripping it tighter and slowly began to move his hand faster as he sucked and excited me until I began to tremble and start to buck my hips up and finally erupted in his mouth. I saw the cheek of his face get pushed out a little as he moved the sperm round inside and then saw it move in as he sucked and knew that he was swallowing my semen.

He finally lifted his head up off of me and gave the head a final kiss before moving up the bed and kissing me on the lips and then moved off for me to get up out of bed.

'I'll have my shower when I get back from the run,' I said as I rummaged through my suitcase which had been under the bed, pulling out some shorts and running shoes, getting my bum stroked by grandad as I pulled the shorts on before putting on my shoes. I gave grandad a kiss as I then called for Tom who came bounding into the room, with his sixth sense guessed that he would be going out, jumped up at me as I then led him out for us to have this run.

Out of the garden gate I turned left and it was only about a hundred yards to the edge of the sector that grandad lived and it was a left turn to start to climb up a small hill and along the ridge between that and another hill I ran with Tom keeping pace with me. We carried on running over rather rough ground up to where there was a small reservoir and on round this and down onto flat ground where Tom was now in his element as he was able to chase some rabbits.

The sun was quite hot even though it had only just risen and I was soon sweating away and was glad to be on the homeward turn knowing that my running hour was up. We got back to the house, Tom now really looking exhausted and panting heavily and as soon as we got inside, he went straight to his water bowl and nearly emptied it, so I had to refill it for him.

Grandad was there in the kitchen and just putting the kettle on for coffee.

'Only be a tick grandad,' I said, giving him a kiss on the cheek and went straight into the bedroom, stripping off my shorts and shoes and went under the blissful shower of cool water. I was back inside ten minutes wearing my sarong and we had breakfast. 'It's a lovely morning out there grandad. Just right for sun bathing and swimming in the pool.'

'Where did you go?' he asked.

'I'll show you,' I said, getting up and going to the kitchen door, which was open. 'There,' I said, pointing to the two hills that we could see above the few houses between us. 'Up there and along over the other one and round the reservoir. Tom enjoyed it in chasing rabbits,' and grinned. 'He didn't catch one, mores the pity, 'cos we could have had a rabbit stew.'

'Well he looks knackered,' grandad said, looking at Tom lying down in the shade in the garden. 'Go and get your book and join him while I wash up.' This I did plus a towel and was soon down on the lounger. 'Only an hour in the sun Toby,' grandad shouted down and it wasn't long before he was down beside me on the other lounger, him with a book too. He also had brought down two beers which we drank and I really hadn't needed to be told about the sun, for after one hour it was too hot, but it wasn't under the umbrella we went, but up to the bedroom.

It was lovely with us being naked on the bed again and I got to fuck him twice before we had a snack lunch and it was back down to the pool were I spent quite some time swimming up and down while he rested under the shade of the umbrella.

We had dinner early and back to bed we went where I was able to fuck him twice again and sucked on him in between as well as sucking on his shaved balls while he played with mine. That was the pattern for the first week with the morning run with Tom, fucking grandad twice in the morning and the same at night with sunbathing and swimming in between.

We had to do some shopping and it was down to the town's market and he kept quiet for me to talk to the stall holders in Spanish and did very well, getting all that we wanted with them fully understanding everything that I asked for.

'Well done Toby,' grandad said, patting my back when we'd bought all that we wanted. 'I think you got all that stuff cheaper than I would. I think that with me and others I might add, when speaking English, charge us more than a local Spaniard.' He then took me off to a restaurant where we had the menu of the day lunch which was quite cheap and it was sunbathing that afternoon and noticed that I was turning a nice brown already.

We also went swimming one evening when it was dark and had the pool light on but then was surprised when he turned it off and jumped into the pool by me.

'I've always wanted to have a fuck in the pool,' grandad said, giving my bum a stroke and I put my hand down and found that he was up hard in spite of the cool water. So in the shallow end where the water level only reached up to my navel, I bent over and held the side of the pool and had the pleasure of having his cock slide up into me and had him fuck me. I was surprised at how erotic it was when he was bent over and I pushed my erect cock up into his ass, going from the cool water into the heat of his body and getting the different changes in the moving of myself in and out of his back passage. It was lovely and enjoyed it so much that I didn't last long before I was holding his hips firmly as I rammed my body up to his, coming inside to his little cries of delight at every shot of my sperm that he claimed to have felt. We then sat on the underwater bench and washed our cocks before getting out to dry ourselves before going to bed where I was able to fuck him twice again and then have me sucking on his cock and balls.

=oOo=

It was a lovely five and a half weeks I had with grandad, getting to fuck him at least three times a day with him fucking me every other day and the sucking of each other, though not remembering how many times we did this to each other. In between times, we would kiss and stroke each other, both of us as brown as berries, my tan being a lovely golden colour while his was a deep brown, well, he'd been out here much longer than me.

It's strange that the first week with him, the time seemed quite long, whereas that last week seemed to fly by and on that last night in his bed, we both cried as we had sex for I would be leaving the next day. We had gone to bed early for he wanted me to fuck him as many times that I could and he even managed to fuck me twice as opposed to me fucking him six times. It must have been about four in the morning before we went to sleep, holding each other as we kissed and cried with it being our last night.

We made love slowly that morning, him on his knees with me up behind him. Slowly moving myself back and forth inside that tight orifice that I just loved putting my dick into. My tears dropping onto his lower back at this last fucking that we would have and he was crying after I pulled out and he went down on me even though I hadn't washed myself, such was the state he was in.

We took our time in the shower, gently washing each other, our tears being washed away with the spraying water. We were at a loss for words as we dressed and I packed my suitcase and when ready to leave, cried again as I hugged Tom, giving him a kiss on his wet nose before I finally said goodbye to him and went out with grandad to the car to be taken to the airport. We were both so choked up with our own emotions that we didn't speak for the whole journey until he finally brought the car to a stop in the airport's car park, where I then pulled him into my arms.

'I love you grandad,' I whispered into his ear. 'I wish I could stay here forever with you.'

'I wish that too Toby,' he said, his voice as thick as mine and I could see that he was having difficulty in holding back the tears. 'I'm going to miss you. Not only for the pleasure that we've had together but your company as well.'

'Can I come again?' I asked, the tears now rolling down my cheeks.

'You can come anytime you wish,' he said and gave out a shaky laugh. 'And cum into me as often as you like.' I laughed at the pun and gave him the biggest kiss I could before we got out of the car. He insisted that he carry my suitcase into the airport to join the queue until my case was weighed and disappeared out of sight. My boarding paper had been checked and it was only the passport control to go through now.

We stopped just before it and went into each other's arms for a final hug and shared the Gaelic kiss before we broke apart and I went through the passport check and turned and gave him a wave that he returned before I went off to the waiting lounge. There I sat, as miserable as sin, running the past five and a half weeks through my mind of the fun we had in bed together. Loving the tightness of him as I moved my erection inside of him, hearing his cries of delight when he felt my sperm coating his inside making my moving more smoothly as I fucked him. The other joy was when he was doing it to me and then the sucking of each other's cock and balls and of the shaving of his. I was really missing him.

We, that is myself and the other passengers, answered the call to board our plane and it wasn't long before we were in the air and two and half hours later, landed in England where mum was waiting for me. She cried with delight as she kissed me and I cried that it wasn't grandad kissing me, and it wasn't long before we were back home.

=oOo=

The following evening, we had a man called Alex have dinner with us and I'm not that stupid not to quickly realise that he was mum's boyfriend. You could tell by the way they looked at each other and guessed that he had slept over while I was away with grandad. This gave me the chance to get across to mum what I wanted to do, so after Alex had left, I had a long chat with mum. At first she denied sleeping with Alex but finally wore her down to admit she was very fond of him and him with her and that he had stayed over some nights.

I carried this on the next day, that being a Sunday so I had to get her to agree my plan for I was back off to college the next day. The basis of what wasn't really an argument, but finally got her to agree that I was prepared to move out when I finished at college and go to live with grandad so that she and Alex could then live together without me being in the way. Mum's objection was along the lines of me having to work for a living as I couldn't expect grandad to pay for my food etc. I countered this with that I was now quite fluent in Spanish, it wouldn't be hard for me to get a job. Then she threw up about my college and my getting my degree which I countered with saying that as soon as I got it, I would leave. That could cause trouble she argued and I said that all she had to tell them was that I had left the country and couldn't be contacted.

I finally got her to agree with a subtle bit of blackmailing in respect of Alex. He came round for Sunday lunch and I could see his eyes light up when I casually told him that in three months' time I would be moving out to live in Spain with my grandfather, so I got him on my side as it were. I was a happy bunny going back to college knowing that it would only be for three months.

Grandad had his seventieth birthday and we sent him his cards and presents saying that we were sorry that we couldn't be there with him, though I added a little bit more into my card to him and knew that he wouldn't let other people read it.

Next was my birthday a month later which Alex went and paid for a good night out to celebrate me reaching twenty. I think he did this by knowing that in another month I would have left home and he could move in to be with mum. Then came the end of this half of term and didn't tell anyone at school that I wouldn't be returning. I had saved up enough money to buy a one way plane ticket to Spain and the day soon arrived when I said my goodbye to both mum and Alex, her crying at my leaving but mollified her with that it was only a short plane ride away and we would still see each other as we both had our own lives to live. Both of them came with me to the airport where I gave mum a farewell kiss and shook hands with Alex and told him to look after mum and had the pleasure of his face going a little red when he said he would.

On leaving them and in the waiting area, I used a phone there and phoned grandad.

'Hello grandad,' I began when the connection was made. 'I don't have much time to speak. My plane takes off in thirty minutes. Can you pick me up at the airport at half three?'

'Er…' he stammered. 'Er…yes Toby.'

'I've left home and mum understands that I was only leaving so that she could then get closer to her boyfriend. I love yo……' I'd run out of loose change and was cut off. Those bloody phones there in the airport ate money like nobody's business, they must make a fortune those phone companies.

I was like a cat on a hot tin roof I was so heaped up with excitement, for I was going back to the man I loved and who loved me. That he was my grandad didn't faze me in the slightest. He liked fucking me and I loved fucking him. I also loved sucking on his cock and balls and him sucking mine. Shit! I loved him more than life itself.

My heart was pounding fit to bust as the plane took off, taking me to grandad and hoped that he would be there when I arrived. He had to be! He loved me! Christ, I lost count of all the reasons that he might send me back home but my mind countered with as many reasons for him to let me stay with him. I fretted the whole two and a half hours until we landed.

It was still pounding away when I collected my suitcase from the revolving carousel and made my way to the exit. Then there he was! Almost hopping about as I got close and when he opened his arms, I flew into them and gave him the biggest hug I could.

'I'm home grandad!'

=oOo=

I couldn't help talking a lot of nonsense the whole trip to his, now our home. How was he? How was Tom? How was everything? I just couldn't stop talking or from stroking his thigh and having him stroke mine, giving me a massive boner that made it uncomfortable to be sitting upright in the passenger seat of the car.

I was bubbling with excitement when we arrived home. I loved that. Home! Grandad's and mine now, too. Tom went apeshit when he saw me. Jumping up and down, racing round the room and me, barking away, his tail moving faster than the eye could follow.

'He missed you as much as I did Toby,' grandad said, shooing Tom away before taking me into his arms. 'Did you miss me too Toby?'

'You don't know how much grandad,' I said to him as I gave him a kiss on the lips. It was more than a kiss I got back in return. It was the unspoken word of heaven that it would be back with my love, the man who I would die for and knew would do the same for me. 'I love you grandad. Let's go to bed and share the love we have.'

He had tears in his eyes as we went into the bedroom where we undressed and with both of us naked, climbed onto the bed and upright on our knees, went into each other's arms and kissed, our erections clashing together as we slowly fell onto our sides without letting go, to kiss and stroke each other until we broke apart for me to turn round on the bed.

What bliss to feel his hot mouth take in the head of my cock as I did the same to him, loving the smell of his body and the taste of his love juice. To suck, tease and chew on that wonderful organ a well as to be massaging it until the nectar was released, to hold in the mouth, to savour the taste before swallowing the life giving seed that was the very essence of love.

By my sucking on grandad, I was depriving myself of having the added pleasure of having him back up inside me for another day but within the hour I was then able to help give him the pleasure of having me up behind and inside him once again. We both cried out with joy as I gave him what he wanted and I from giving it to him and the pleasure of having him.

I fucked him senseless over the rest of the week with him somehow finding the strength to have me at least once a day, filling me with his erection and giving me the joy of having him back inside me. The years fell away from him in our love making and we found it became easier for him to see to me on a more frequent basis.

Christmas came and passed as did the entry into the New Year and winter, though the latter wasn't as harsh or long as that of England and it wasn't long before Spring arrived closely followed by the summer. By then I was already as brown as a berry and nearly the same colour as grandad with catching the early sun. Grandad lost some of his paunch with the exercise we had in bed and even Tom lost weight with our daily morning run. My body grew stronger with my daily swimming, building up my arm and leg muscles though I gave him a lot of my inner strength by pleasuring him in bed to which we seemed to spend most of our time and it wasn't all in sleeping.

'Grandad,' I began one evening just after our fucking of each other. 'I've got to think about getting a job or something soon.'

'Why Toby?' he asked.

'Well I can't keep sponging off you as it were by not putting some money into the kitty.' I said, stroking his chest.

'Nonsense! There's still enough there in the bank to keep us going,' he replied.

'But it's not right grandad that I keep taking from you and not giving anything back,' I said.

'You're already giving me what I want,' he chuckled, his hand stroking my flaccid cock.

'No. I'm serious. I should be out earning some money,' I said.

'Doing what?' grandad asked.

'With me now really speaking Spanish, thought of getting a school job, teaching English and Maths. I was pretty good at that in school,' I answered.

'Ah, we might run into a few problems with that,' grandad said. 'I think you would have to be a resident and all the rest before thinking of taking on a job that a Spaniard could do.'

'Are you trying to put me off?' I asked.

'No, not at all, but it's not going to be as easy as you think,' he replied. So that was that for the time being as with his playing and stroking of me had aroused me and pulled me onto him and kissed me. 'For now, let me have what I really want from you,' he said with a grin and I couldn't help but smile back at him and rolled off for him to assume the position he favoured and for me to get up behind him and have the pleasure and joy of pushing my erect cock up into his backside, to have the tightness completely surround my now throbbing piece of meat and move in and out of him till I cummed, giving him my sperm which made him give out cries of delight at every spray that hit his insides. My joy was coming inside him and giving him pleasure as I had mine.

One of his major delights in us having sex was when we used one of the hard back chairs in the dining area where I sat down with my erection held upright for him to straddle my thighs and lower himself down onto it until he was sitting on my thighs with my cock throbbing inside him. This way we could hold each other and kiss as he moved himself up and down on my shaft in the fucking of himself. Quite often he would have an emission with his cock being masturbated between our chests for him to come and what we could lick off afterwards.

=oOo=

It took a couple of months for me to become a resident and get papers to obtain work, getting all this done without having to have an interpreter as my Spanish was fluent enough to get things moving faster than not knowing the language. The downcast side of me seeking work at a school was the timing. Another thing was that grandad paid for me to take driving lesson for a small motor bike, something like the old Vespa which wasn't any kind of racing machine and was old enough for riding one of these things. Grandad surprised me again by buying one for me when I passed my driving test. Boy didn't he get a really right fucking session from me that night as my way of thanking him. Come to think of it, I thanked him every night in having me with him. Take that pun whichever way you like, but he preferred the way that we had sex.

But on making enquiries found no places vacant but maybe the following year there could be one, but with a bit of advertising, managed to bring a little money in by doing interpretations and assisting some of the English population of where we lived. I got more people asking for me for I was charging the cheapest hourly rate or a fixed price depending on what was wanted.

It was lovely to spend a lot of time with grandad down by the pool, keeping the sun tan going as well as the swimming and having finally read all of his books and those that he was still writing, that I went and re-read them. Even after reading for the second time would still give me erections that he wanted to share with me and so we also spent more of our time in bed together. I think I've mentioned this before about our time spent in or on our bed. Considering that you normally spend eight hours of twenty four sleeping leaving you with sixteen hours of the day. I reckoned on three hours in the morning. Another three in the afternoon and going to bed early for at least four hours before sleeping. So only six hours were used in eating, shopping, washing etc. It quite exhausted grandad all this time that we spent in bed.

It was the approach of my twenty first birthday that grandad suggested that we had mum and her boyfriend over to celebrate it with us.

'You and Alex can have my bed and I'll bed down with grandad,' I told her. 'Just like that Christmas we spent here,' laughing to myself at me coming out with this when I had only ever once slept in that bed upstairs, that being on my first visit and meeting of grandad.

They came over for three days and enjoyed the visit, grandad having chuckled when I said about me having to sleep with him while they were with us. It went off well, mum pleased that with me being with grandad and enjoying myself by living with him and letting her get on with her life with Alex.

After seeing them off at the airport it was back to the two of us again being able to resort to our having sex whenever we wanted during the day in addition to that which we shared at night. Now was the time to see if I could be taken on as a teacher in one of the two schools in town and we were both surprised when the headmaster of the first would be delighted with me becoming a teacher of English in the first one that I had gone and spoken to. That was because English was now on the curriculum of schools in Spain and with me really proficient in the language, wanted me to start at the beginning of the New Year's term. All my Spanish papers were in order and was impressed with my Open University diplomas in both the language and maths.

Grandad and I celebrated this at one of the area's most expensive restaurants and there's no need to say how we carried on the celebration in bed that night. Fuck it, I will tell you! Grandad surpassed himself in his kissing every part of my body, even going as far as rimming my ring piece, something he had never done before, having his tongue go where it was normally his erect cock. Needless to say I returned the pleasure threefold by having him that many times in the fucking of him though it was still only the once with him fucking me. In between bouts, it was the sucking and fondling of balls and got round to shaving him for the second time which was later. I even had him shave mine that was now producing more hair than needed.

=oOo=

It was with some trepidation that I set out from home on my little bike to be introduced to the rest of the teaching staff on my first day there but they quickly put me at ease with me being able to speak their language so fluently. The same with my first class and found it quite easy by following the way I had learned Spanish, though the other way round this time. The Math class was a breeze as in both of my starting classes were of the youngest pupils, but I survived and had been quite pleased with the reception that I got from all the classes that I dealt with on that first day. Grandad was pleased for me too and showed it in bed that night.

I got on well with the rest of the staff of the school and I found that most of them, the males, were in the late forties in age and one was only three years older than myself, so we tended to spend some of our free time talking to each other. His name was Ramon Perez and it didn't take long to learn that his home had been in Madrid and that he now lived in a rented apartment in town on his own and it didn't take a crystal ball to understand that he was a lonely man and guessed that the reason for him to leave his home in Madrid was that he was gay. I was quick to pick up the nuances of his feelings, like the gentle touch of the hand when speaking to me and emphasising a point and of the way he looked at me when speaking.

'It's nice to have someone younger to talk to,' he told me. 'Someone closer to my age.' Now you must remember that he is Spanish and that is the language we used, well, all of my talking in school was in Spanish, but I have, for your convenience, have translated it into English. We would often eat together during the siesta break, which was from two till four in the afternoon, where he told me quite a bit about himself. Now I would take a packed lunch with me, but he started bringing in food that he had cooked for me to try and share his lunch. His was a bit shorter than me and not as well built as me but had a lovely smile in his dark face. Well not that dark but looking like he had a good sun tan being more brown that dark. His hair was black and he had brown eyes that made me think that they were not far off like that of Tom. White teeth and a habit of often running the tip of his tongue over his lips.

I'd been there about two months when he asked if I would like to have an evening meal with him at his place. I begged off saying that my dinner would be ready for me when I got home. He already knew that I was living out of town with my grandad but still asked if I would another day. I managed to not say yes or no at that time, for I wanted to speak to grandad before saying anymore.

'Grandad,' I began when we were in bed that night after me having fucked him and then sucked on him, both of which we enjoyed and were now just stroking each other. 'You know I've spoken of the other teachers at the school?' To which he nodded. 'Well Ramon has asked me to have an evening meal with him sometime in the near future and I don't know whether to accept or not.'

'Well that's up to you Toby,' he replied.

'It's…it's not the meal grandad, it's…it's just that I get the impression from the way he speaks and the occasional touch that…that he wants more than just having my company for dinner.' Grandad was quite blunt.

'You think he wants sex?'

'Er...well, yes,' I stammered.

'Toby,' he began, coming up onto his elbow and leaning on his side as he looked at me. 'You are a man now. Young. Healthy and fit, and quite a handsome man at that. I think that you would attract men as well as women. You should really mix with persons closer to your age than keep with an old man like me.'

'You're not an old man to me grandad,' I cried.

'Face the fact that I am Toby. Have dinner with him and if he wants sex, go ahead,' he said.

'You...you'd let me have sex with someone else?' I asked, a tremor running through my body which I was sure he could feel.

'Yes. Sex is good with either a man or woman. Only if you do, always use a condom and come back home to me, for I love you so much Toby that it would break my heart if you now left me,' he said and in the gloom of the room, I could see tears in his eyes.

'Oh grandad. I love you too. So much that it hurts,' I cried, moving up myself to roll him onto his back to kiss him. A passionate one to try and show him just how much I did love him.

'I can feel what hurts the most,' he chuckled, him speaking of my erection that was pressing against his thigh. 'Let's stop that hurting first.' I couldn't help but grin back at him, really wanting to fuck him and show how much I needed him. We parted and he turned round and got up onto his knees while I got onto mine and shuffled round him and got in between his open legs and surprised him by bending down my head and kissing each cheek of his bum before tonguing his ass. This made him shiver at him feeling what my tongue was doing, putting down some saliva for I was going to fuck him bare back, which we now did most of the time when we had each other.

With him now used to having my cock up inside him, there wasn't any pain though he still gave out a grunt and a groan as I widened his ring piece as the head of my cock slowly expanded him before it slipped in to feel his body heat and have his muscle flex itself round the head before I moved and pushed the rest of my pulsating cock into the tightness of his orifice.

'I love you grandad,' I whispered as I moved myself back and forth inside him. I didn't know that he had heard the whisper.

'I love you too Toby,' he said. 'Even more so when you are where you are now.'

It wasn't long before I was holding him firmly in my hands as I began to have my orgasm and came, quite copiously inside him to his cries of delight at feeling my sperm hit his insides. Then came his cry of dismay when I pulled out and got off the bed to go and wash myself and on returning, went down and sucked on his lovely cock. I say lovely for it was in all aspects whether it was hard or soft as were his balls which he liked me taking them into my mouth to suck.

We kissed and cuddled afterwards before he spoke of what we had talked about earlier.

'If you do accept his offer for dinner, give me a ring early so as not to waste food and fret that you haven't arrived home at the usual time.'

CHAPTER X

That I did the next day for Ramon asked me again if I would like dinner at his place and I accepted. With the children leaving the school, we went to my bike where I had a spare helmet in the box that was under the seat and with him behind me, (I chuckled at this thought), his hands round my waist, drove off to his place which wasn't far and he usually walked to school.

It was a single bed apartment and so small and it would have fitted into our place and still have plenty of room. The lounge, if it could be called that, so small that a two seat sofa, a television, a little bookcase and a table with two chairs, filled the room. It had a kitchenette that only one person could work inside it so didn't deserve the name kitchen and later saw the bedroom that was so small it only had room for a single bed. The bathroom, well, it could only just take the toilet, a wash basin and a narrow shower cubicle instead of a bath.

He told me to sit either at the table or the sofa while he prepared and cooked our dinner. I opted for the table where I could see him do this and he poured out some red wine from a container that you could get refilled at the bodega. That is a shop that sells all drinks and only costs about a pound to fill a litre container from big vats. I can't remember the name he gave the meal, meat balls and some kind of spaghetti with strawberries and cream afterwards.

'It's lovely to be able to cook a meal and have somebody else eat with me,' Ramon said as we ate and I found it quite enjoyable. We also drank the whole litre of wine between us and declined my help at my offer to wash up.

'Thank you for coming,' he said as he gave my thigh a stroke. I had to smother the chuckle at his choice of words and took note of his hand that had stroked me which had been easy to reach our chairs being so close together at that small table. We rose up from the table for him the clear away our plates and I could see that he was too shy as to what he should say or do, so I took the bull by the horns. Well we are in Spain after all.

'Can I really thank you Ramon for such a wonderful meal,' giving my lips a caress with my tongue, copying his habit. He wasn't quite sure what or how I was going to thank him, wondering if I was just going to shake his hand and say goodbye. But there wasn't any alarm or rebuff when I took him into my arms and kissed him. His body had been tense when I first touched him but I felt his body relax in my arms and his then went round to hold me tight as he returned the kiss.

'Oh Toby,' he breathed into my ear as we held each other close. Close enough for us both to feel that we had an erection each. 'I've wanted to kiss you from the very first time I saw you.'

'Just a kiss?' I asked of him, looking into his deep brown eyes that were really shining, 'or were there more thoughts in your mind?' I'm sure that my eyes were twinkling at the thought that he wanted me as much as I wanted him at this moment.

'There were lots Toby. Too many to say which was to the fore,' he said, still holding me in a tight embrace and I'm sure I felt his cock twitch.

'Would one of them being of us two, making love to each other?' I asked, making my cock twitch in answer to his.

'Oh yes Toby, yes,' he breathed out in a kind of sigh as his eyes closed and he kissed me. It was all uphill from that point. We broke apart and he led me into his small bedroom where we fumbled in getting each other's clothes off until we were both naked. Our erections up and hard sticking out from our groins, his had been circumcised the same as grandad's and was pleased to note that mine was bigger than his. Not a lot, but bigger.

We got onto the narrow bed and cuddled and kissed. We had to lie on our sides for it wasn't wide enough for both of to lie on our backs side by side.

'Fuck me Toby,' he breathed into my mouth. 'I've been dreaming of you being on my bed and fucking me.'

'Well let's make the dream come true. Do you have any condoms?' I asked in reply. If he hadn't, I had two in my trousers bringing them along just in case he hadn't, but he did and quickly got them from the small bedside cabinet drawer.

I had to get up onto my knees as he did too and bent down and took the head of my cock into his mouth. It was hot and felt his tongue move round and over it and I found that there wasn't any difference between his mouth and that of grandad's except that grandad really knew how to use his tongue. It was only a brief suck for he quickly got a condom out of its wrapper and rolled it over the head and down the shaft of my cock before lying down on his back on the bed. Which indicated the position he wanted to be fucked in.

His legs were open and he lifted them up for me to get in between them and had his legs come up and onto my shoulders as I moved in closer and when my hands were on either side of his body, they slipped down a little and he used them against my arms to lift up his lower half.

I must say that even without seeing my target, he was at the right level for the head of my covered cock to unerringly hit the target. I looked at his face to see his smile, showing his white teeth as I began to push myself up into his tight ass. He gave a grimace at being widened but then gave a big grin as the head slipped in and gave out a gasp as I pushed as much of myself into him. His muscle was moving like mad around my cock as I began to move and fuck him.

'Aaah. It's big Toby,' he gasped. 'But lovely. It's been a long time since I had a cock inside me and definitely not as big as yours.'

It was nice having my body at full stretch, my arms keeping his legs up as my hips kept moving to have my shaft slide back and forth inside that tight and hot hole of his. As much as I loved being where I was in the fucking of another man, my mind was giving out apologies to grandad that I was using my erect cock to fuck another person and not him. Was I being unfaithful in doing this? My mind said no for he had given his permission, but it still made me feel guilty.

I hadn't been inside Ramon that long before I started to cum, and cum I did and thought that I was going to burst the condom it felt that there was so much filling the little rubber bulb at the end of it. Ramon's eyes were shining at feeling the expansion of my cock as it threw my semen into him. His arms rose up when I came to a stop and so I slowly eased my body down onto his, squashing his erection between us and having his legs slide down my arms and it must have felt as though I was splitting him in two until I was full length on him with my cock still inside him, throbbing away. We kissed with some passion and had his tongue pushing against my teeth for me to open my mouth for a French kiss.

But his body began easing and that with this action, I was slowly slipping out of him and it was only when it was right out did I lift myself up from lying on top of him.

'Oh Toby, that was lovely. Never had I ever had a man like you,' he said with a beautiful smile on his face and as I sat back on my heels, he rose up and shifting his body, leaned down and pulled the condom off me and took the head of my sperm coated cock and sucked out any leftovers as well as licking me clean.

Then it was my turn to be fucked and went into the same position on my back and had his covered cock pushed up into me as my legs rested on his shoulders. He wasn't as big as grandad but what the fuck. A fuck was a fuck and it was a cock inside me where I loved having one and crooned as I felt him moving inside and giving me that internal massage. His face was all smiles as he looked at me as he moved and I loved it, both the smiles and having him fuck me. But he didn't last long either before he was trying to get more of himself inside me as he shot his load into the rubber before coming to a stop to slide down and lie on top of me for us to kiss. I tried to hold his cock inside of me with my sphincter muscle but couldn't stop the inevitability of it sliding out.

Like him, I quickly got the condom off his still hard erection and sucked on him getting my first taste of a Spaniards sperm and found it not unlike that of grandad. Slightly salty and having a mild flavour to it that wasn't unpleasant to the tongue.

With us now parted from our copulation, we kissed each for a little while before I told him that it was time for me to be leaving which brought tears to his eyes, but understood that I had to go home sometime. So we left the bed and in the narrow space available, got dressed and when back in the only other room, we held each other as I thanked him for such a lovely meal and what we had for dessert which made him grin, though it didn't stop the tears from rolling down his cheeks as we said a final farewell.

It was an exhilarated me that rode my bike home. Home to grandad who no doubt would begin to worry if I was too late and no doubt would want to know the ins and outs of me being with Ramon. I arrived home and took the bike through the double gates and down to the under build beneath the house to where I parked it out of sight before going up into the house.

'I'm home grandad,' I called out.

'I know,' I heard his voice from the kitchen. 'Tom told me. He knows the sound of your bike.' I went round to the kitchen where he was doing some washing up, and gave him a kiss.

'Well?' he asked with a smile on his face.

'Well what?' I replied, keeping my face straight.

'You know damn well what. How was your dinner with this Ramon?'

'Very good considering,' I replied.

'Did you?' him not having to finish the question.

'Er…sort of,' I stammered.

'What kind of answer is that? Sort of! Did he want you to fuck him?'

'Er…sort of,' I stammered again.

'For fuck's sake Toby! Did you fuck him or not?' he cried out with an exasperated expression on his face.

'Yes!' I cried out. 'But it was nowhere as good as with you.'

'Flattery will get you everywhere,' he said wiping his hands. 'So where would you like to go?'

'Now that's a stupid question grandad,' I said with a grin, rubbing my crotch.

'Okay,' he laughed, throwing the towel aside and moved off to the bedroom with me following him, a smile on my face. It didn't take us long to get our clothes off and get onto the bed to move into each other's arms to hug and kiss.

So I gave him a full blow by blow account of the sex I had with Ramon and finding that during the telling, he became aroused and had his cock up nice and hard. I moved down the bed and took him into my mouth. It wasn't often he was up as hard as this and it gave me greater pleasure in sucking on him instead of it being half limp.

'That's enough Toby, enough,' he cried, tugging at my ears. 'I'd rather have you now while I'm still able.'

'That's the spirit grandad,' I said, moving off of him and getting up onto my knees. He moved and got behind and in between my legs.

'He did use a condom Toby?' he asked, one hand holding my hip.

'We both did grandad, so you can still fuck me bare back,' I told him.

'That's my boy,' he said as he quickly pushed himself up into my ass. I grunted at the suddenness of him entering me but drooled at the mouth that it was once again my grandad's lovely big cock ploughing into me. 'Christ! It hasn't been this big for a long time,' I gasped, now really feeling him throb and move inside me. It was lovely the way he moved it, much better than the way Ramon did, moving his hips from side to side and felt that he was really screwing me. He even lasted longer in having me and though he didn't give me as much semen, it was almost double that what he had been giving me over the past few months. I even cried out that I felt him cum inside me as he came to a stop, still twitching his cock and causing more saliva to drip from my mouth.

Well he's sown his oats I said to myself as that hated part of having sex this way was losing that wonderful cock that had been such a pleasure to have reaming my inside channel. But out it was and fell onto my side to watch him leave the bed to go and wash himself. That didn't take long and he was soon on the bed next to me.

'Now it's my turn to have what Ramon had,' he said, moving up onto his knees.

'He laid on his back, grandad, not on his knees,' I said, not moving as yet.

'Well I'd rather have it this way. You know it hurts my back the other way,' he said, getting his legs apart. 'Well, come on, I'm waiting.'

'Okay grandad,' I said, now moving and getting behind him, stroking his bum as I did so. Boy, did I make him give out a cry as I rammed myself up into as he had done to me, but it was grand to be back in this saddle again, fucking my one and only love up the ass.

'Wow! You feel bigger too,' he gasped in between my thrusts, liking what I was doing, and because it hadn't been long since I had been fucking Ramon, I was able to last a bit longer which pleased us both until I cummed, giving him the seed that had regenerated inside my balls. I knew by his little cry that he had felt me cumming, knowing also by the slight expansion of the cock head and extra throb that ran through the shaft. He too gave out the same cry as I did when I pulled out to go and wash myself.

'You can fuck him again,' grandad said as we kissed and cuddled when I was back on the bed, 'if you are going to be as big as that which I've just had.'

'You don't mind then?' I asked, stroking his hairless chest.

'No, but only once a week if you are going to continue to do so. I miss you in bed in the afternoon with you being in school so I'll expect it to be at least twice a night in future. I do really miss you during the day too and it's only the thought of us being in bed together at night that keeps me going throughout the day.'

'Okay grandad,' I said. 'If you play with my cock and balls, you might be able to bring it up to its fighting strength.'

'I don't know which of us is becoming more of a slut in wanting a hard cock for our pleasure,' he said with a grin as he started on the chore, question that word, in raising the dead. Which he did for me to fuck him again.

=oOo=

It then began a pattern where I would have dinner once a week with Ramon and of course going into his bedroom for us to fuck each other though I had to admonish him to stop his touching of me while in school as the other teachers might start making comments. I would then get home on those days and fuck grandad at least twice that same evening before falling asleep. The weekends were best for grandad with me being home all day so that we could have sex in different ways in the morning, afternoon and evening as well as during the night if aroused.

Now I don't know which of us brought up the subject of sex with Ramon, no, wait a minute, it was grandad. Now I remember. He had asked me if I thought that Ramon would like to try us making it a threesome some night. Now this brought me up to having an instant erection. Being fucked and having a cock to suck on at the same time? It sounded as though it would be great.

'You mean bring Ramon home one day?' I asked him.

'Yes. He might like it.'

'You randy bugger! You want to be fucked twice as many times than I can do to you,' I exclaimed. He had the decency to give me an unashamed smile as he nodded his head.

'He might not want to,' I countered.

'Well there's no harm in asking, is there?' he said. 'If it was during the week, he could stay overnight and travel on the back of your bike to school in the morning.' Now I'd been having dinner and then sex with Ramon on a Friday, so what he said had made sense, if he wanted to stay the night too. So on that next Friday after us having had each other after dinner, I asked him if he would like to meet my grandfather and if he was agreeable, we three could have sex together. You would have thought that I was offering him the moon for his eyes had lit up like a beacon at the suggestion and was all for it. I said about it being during the week so that he could ride with me to school the following day. I think grandad was delighted too when I told him that Ramon would be with us on the following Wednesday.

The day came round and I had butterflies in my stomach hoping that grandad and Ramon would hit it off.

'Nervous?' I asked Ramon as we put on our helmets prior to getting on the bike to go home for dinner, and hopefully, sex with the three of us.

'Yes Toby,' he replied in English. He was learning quite a bit from me now. 'I…,' and then had to revert back to Spanish. 'I hope that he will like me and that we can all have fun tonight.'

'That we will,' I told him in the same language. So off we set and it was only a twenty five minute run before we arrived and with the bike put away, we went into the house to be greeted by Tom first.

'Qué perro encantador,' Ramon exclaimed, giving Tom several strokes of his head.

'Yes, he is a lovely dog,' I replied, for that was what he had said. 'Now meet grandad ,' and led him inside. 'Hello grandad,' I greeted him and went into a hug and kissed him. I deliberately kissed grandad in front of Ramon to let him know that we were indeed lovers, which I had told him some time ago in our relationship.

'Grandad, this is Ramon. Ramon this is abuelito,' I said in introducing them. Abuelito is grandad in Spanish.

'Buenas noches Señor,' Ramon said, holding his hand out which grandad shook before taking him into his arms and greeting him the Spanish way with a pressing of both cheeks.

'Welcome to my home Ramon,' was his reply.

Now with Ramon's English being very limited, for the sake of continuity will put down Ramon's words in English though most of them I did translate for the benefit of grandad.

'This is a lovely house, er, grandad,' Ramon said. Him being told at the outset that grandad was what he was known as. 'It's a much better place than where I now live.'

'Thank you Ramon. Home is what you make it,' grandad replied going to the drinks cabinet. 'You're a fine looking young man,' he said with a smile and knew that he was mentally stripping him as he looked Ramon over. 'Now what would like to drink with your dinner?' Ramon replied that he would drink what we would have.

The table had already been laid out for three and grandad poured out some red wine into the glasses there before telling us to sit down while he served us our meal. It was a lovely meal being half-Spanish and half-English, it being a prawn cocktail to start followed by a pot roast and finished off with a crème brulee. Two bottles of wine were drunk before we had finished and Ramon's offer to help in the washing up afterwards was politely refused.

'Grandad will want you to fuck him first when we go to bed,' I told Ramon as we sat together on the sofa with a drink in our hands, waiting for grandad to finish the washing up. Which wasn't long before he came into the lounge with a big smile on his face.

'Toby has told me that you've got a lovely body,' he said to Ramon, making him blush. 'I can't wait to see it.' Ramon looked to me and I gave him a grin.

'Let's go to bed then Ramon and let him see how right I was,' I said as I put my empty glass down and held out my hand to him. He hastily finished his drink and putting his glass down, took my hand and stood up for me to lead him to the bedroom followed by grandad.

Ramon was acting rather shyly, so I quickly got my clothes off for him to see that I now had an erection as he slowly began to take his off. Grandad had also started undressing and was as naked as me, showing that he too had an erection. Ramon finally got his clothes off and proved that he was ready for sex for his cock was fully erect and sticking out from his groin.

'That's a lovely looking cock Ramon,' said grandad getting on the bed. 'Can I give it a welcome kiss and suck?' Somewhat red in the face at the bluntness of grandad, got onto the bed and lay on his back with me then getting on alongside of him so that he was in the middle. Grandad wasn't slow in moving down and taking Ramon's erection into his mouth. Ramon gave out a groan that I stifled by leaning over him and giving him an open mouthed kiss as I ran my hand up and down his chest as grandad sucked on him. It was only for a few minutes of this before grandad lifted his head up.

'You got such a lovely cock Ramon. Will you fuck me with it?' he asked, his eyes positively gleaming. I didn't wait for any answer, and quickly opened a condom wrapper and grandad and me got the rubber down over Ramon's erection before we all moved round on the bed for grandad to get up onto his knees and Ramon to position himself behind him. I'm sure my eyes were gleaming too as I grinned at Ramon and nodded my head as if to say well go ahead and fuck him. He gave me a smile back and put his hands onto grandad's hips as I moved down the bed and watched as his covered cock was slowly pushed up into grandad's backside.

Grandad gave out a little cry as his asshole was widened and then a gasp as I watched Ramon's cock disappear into grandad until his thighs were tight up to the cheeks of grandad. I was tempted to slide under grandad to take his throbbing cock into my mouth to suck, but refrained, for I knew that he would like to fuck Ramon with it, so I didn't. Instead, I fondled Ramon's balls as he moved himself in and out of grandad's ass.

'Harder Ramon, harder,' he panted which didn't need translating and gave out gasps as we had the sounds of Ramon's thighs smacking up to grandad's cheeks, me letting go of his balls for them to do the same as they swung back and forth. It wasn't long before Ramon straightened up and just let his hips twitch as he cummed inside the condom, getting little cries of delight from grandad as he felt the expanding cock head give out the emissions from Ramon.

'That was fucking lovely,' grandad panted as Ramon came to a halt, breathing heavily as he leaned in towards grandad's rear for a moment or two before pulling out. Grandad gave out a groan at the losing of that cock from his ass.

'Stay there grandad, for I'm next,' I said as I rolled a condom down over my erection, but then leaned in towards Ramon first to pull off his condom and sucked on the wet head of his cock to suck out what was left of his sperm and licked the head clean before releasing him to move out of the way for me to get behind grandad for my turn. Grandad was over the moon at having this second male organ being inserted into him and give him the same pleasure all over again at having another hard cock ream his insides.

He loved it as I moved inside him and I loved being in the tightness of his backside, there not being any difference between his and Ramon's in this respect except for the different rate of the flexing of the inside muscle around the shaft of my cock. I soon came into the condom to the little cries of delight from beneath me and when I pulled out, Grandad pointed to Ramon to do the honours in the cleaning up process of sucking out any residual sperm. Grandad, now lying on his side, grinning at me as well as watching Ramon suck on my dick.

'Well I've only got one shot with my cannon,' grandad said as he lay together, 'so who's it to be?'

'As you've had me before, let Ramon have the honour of finding out what a prick you are,' then giggled. 'Sorry. What a prick *you've* got.' They both laughed at this "cock" up in what I had said. So Ramon got into position and I had the pleasure of hearing Ramon give out a cry as grandad pushed his weapon into him and give out grunts as grandad fucked him. I let him suck on grandad after he had pulled out and I left the bed to go and get us a beer each to drink while waiting for us two studs to recover and replenish our balls with some fresh semen.

Ramon got the most kisses between us, it being his first time in bed with grandad though I didn't go without. It was also awkward we found out as to which pair of balls to play with in the attempts to make our cocks rise up enough for another session. It was finally achieved, well for Ramon and myself as grandad could only rise to half-mast.

It was now the three of us to be coupled together. Grandad went onto his knees and Ramon got between his open legs and pushed himself inside grandad. With him firmly embedded inside his ass, he leaned over his lower back for me to then give Ramon my erection, which moved in nicely thank you. So with us all joined up, I became the moving power and began to fuck Ramon and with my moving his body in this fashion as I fucked him, he was being moved to be able to be fucking grandad. It became difficult to say which one was grunting and who was panting as two backsides were being reamed, Ramon getting the better deal by fucking and being fucked at the same time, though later that night, I got to be in the middle to have the double pleasure of having it both ways.

Overall, the three of us had a fucking good time in bed that night and were all exhausted as we fell asleep in tangled limbs. We were awake early enough for Ramon and myself to fuck grandad, though not having the time to wait for us to be roused enough for each other as we still had to go to school. Grandad, bless him, got up with us to make us a breakfast and at the same time, make something for our lunch.

'I love you grandad,' I said in giving him a kiss before we left and he had the surprise of Ramon saying the same as he gave him a kiss.

'Thank you for having me,' Ramon added and got a chuckle from grandad with him saying this in English.

'It's me also saying thank you for having me too,' he replied and I made Ramon laugh in telling him that what he had said was able of being taken two ways. One being the politeness of being allowed into his home and the other of having had sex together.

Grandad waved us goodbye and later during a break between classes, Ramon said that he liked my grandad and what we had done together the night before and hoped that we could do it again soon.

Back home that night, grandad thanked me for bring Ramon home and sharing him even though it was depriving myself by missing out on some of the sex that we had together. But by taking Ramon home that time was beneficial for grandad for it seemed to rejuvenate him with him now being able to fuck me every night instead of us missing one time in between. He said that he had enjoyed fucking Ramon nearly as much as fucking me and him being able to have the both of us fuck him which was the icing on the cake as far as he was concerned.

'Would you like me to bring him again next week?' I asked him.

'By all means yes. He was good and I think he enjoyed it too,' he said.

'Oh he did and, well he didn't actually say it, but I know that he would like to come again,' and I giggled at the double meaning of my last words.

'Well I would like him to come again,' he laughed, 'not just here but inside me again. That is of course if you don't mind us sharing him and you sharing me. He's got a nice smooth body though not as strong as you are now and I liked stroking him as I do you.'

'Let's then stroke each other in bed after dinner,' I said, which we did, though the stroking of our bodies was low on the list as there were other things to do in bed and that was to be done between our couplings of fucking each other.

=oOo=

From then on, every Wednesday, Ramon came home with me for us to all have sex together, it was great. The question was raised later about seeing if he would move in with us, to which I said no.

'I love Ramon after a fashion, but my love for you grandad is far greater. I don't mind sharing you once a week but I rather us being together for the other nights, and have you all to myself,' I told him.

'You're right Toby. You are my grandson and he is not. You come first. But there will come a time when I will no longer be here and….' I interrupted him.

'Don't say that grandad!' I cried. 'Don't ever say that!' and broke down into tears and had him take me into his arms. 'I don't want to lose you grandad,' I cried as he patted my back.

'I didn't mean to upset you Toby, I'm sorry, but time passes fast now and I've had to think of the future. Your future, not mine. I went to a notary the other day while you were at school and made a new will.'

'I don't want to hear it,' I said, my voice muffled with my head buried in his shoulder.

'Well I'm saying it whether you hear it or not. In the will, I'm leaving the house to you and your mother, now after I'm gone, you can bring Ramon here to live with you if you are still in a relationship with him. It's your future home Toby and I want you to be happy.' I looked up and saw that he had tears running down his face and I buried my face into his shoulder again and sobbed for quite some time.

'I don't ever want you to go grandad. I love you so much I can't bear the thought of you leaving me,' I cried and I was still crying when we went to bed and spent a miserable night even though the sex we had in our joining our bodies together was as good if not better than that of the past. It took me several days to get over this and I gave him as much of my love as I could.

It wasn't long before summer was with us and enabled us to spend the weekends sunbathing and reading his books for with our love secure and me working at school during the week, he was really throwing himself into his writing and he was turning out some really good ones. When one was finished, he would give it to me to proof read and as expected, what with the usual nature of his books, the sexual aspect was quite high and I would get an erection while reading it while on my lounger. So it was off to bed we would go for me to get rid of my erection and to grandad's pleasure, he would be the recipient in the helping by having me fuck him and him to receiving my sperm up inside him.

I loved reading his books and having our sex on a regular basis. We would quite often have sex in a different position for him to be able to write it exactly as he had experienced it, though he still liked it when we used a hard back chair so that we could kiss while having our sex together.

With the summer school break, grandad and I made pigs of ourselves over those weeks between my swimming in the pool and eating where the bed saw more of us than any other place and on this happy note I will finish what my grandad, my lover asked of me so that he could use it in one of his stories.

The End

Here is a sample from another story you may enjoy:

we'd had sex at least a dozen times before I went down and sucked on her.

It was an idyllic last year now having proved myself and having now risen from being a boy into being a man thanks to Betty. Though we promised to write to each other after leaving college, we never did, but I'll always remember her and what she gave me.

Father was pleased at how well I did in respect of my college tuition and accepted the fact that I was joining the army, which I did, and because of my officer's cadet course went in immediately as a second lieutenant. I was then twenty years old and thoroughly enjoyed myself what with the maneuver's and mock battles we did out on Salisbury Plain. I also enjoyed attending the various balls I got invited to by other fellow officers, meeting quite a few pretty women who responded to my charm and let me fuck them, whether it be in bed or having a knee trembler.

There were also parties that I got invited to and it was at one of these that I committed my first act of larceny. The crime being theft. I cannot remember whose house, or really the mansion the party was at, but I'd been taken up to one of the bedrooms by the woman I had been dancing with. In the close bodily contact and being able to almost see all of her tits in the low cut gown she was wearing, I couldn't help but get a hard on.

This she felt and wanted it, hence being almost dragged upstairs into what I can only describe as being a female's boudoir. Quite lavish in its decoration with many frills and drapes and even a four poster bed. It was on this that I fucked this hungry woman whose name I also cannot remember, but it was a nice fuck that we had and it was after we had got dressed and while she was in the bathroom, checking over her make-up, I had started wandering about the room.

I'd opened a wardrobe door and there inside, on a shelf was a large box which I opened to find that it contained quite a few pieces of jewellery. I couldn't resist poking this lot about and picked up a nice diamond bracelet that I took a sudden fancy to and went and slipped it into my pocket before closing the box and wardrobe door before my bed partner returned for us to go back downstairs and join the others.

It was only later back in my quarters that I realised of the enormity of what I had done and decided to get rid of it as soon as possible. The very next day, I went into town and found a pawnshop who gladly took it from me, giving me quite a substantial amount of money for it.

Now, whether it was the thrill of stealing the bracelet or of getting the money when I sold it, I don't know, but I began to do this more often. Just the odd piece here and there whenever the opportunity occurred and later selling it for cash.

There was one jeweller in London, that on my selling him my second piece to him, told me that if I was to bring in more, we could both make quite a lot of money. What he was really implying was that he would act as the fence for me in talking to him all and what I could steal for him to break down or rework into an unrecognisable piece.

Not only were there parties to go to but visits to various places and meeting quite a few people in different occupations. It was one such as this that I met Mavis Trimble, a beautician in a television studio when I had gone with an officer friend who had a sister taking part in a drama being recorded there.

It was in one dressing room where we went and my friend's sister was having her make-up done by one of the two girls in there. Though there were two chairs before the mirrors, only his sister was being seen to and I got chatting to the other girl not at the time, working on another actors face. This was Mavis and we chatted for quite some time and was so struck with her, asked if she had any objections to me calling again to talk further. She didn't and so I made several visits to chat and eventually got her to go out with me.

AMY REDEK

PRISON
Sex Slave
WHAT HAPPENS BEHIND BARS?

Gay HARDCORE

I was seventeen when I had my first woman, a girl that was at the same college. Her name was Elizabeth but generally called Betty, who was a spectator one particular day that I was playing rugby. I was a wingman and managed to get one try in the game that we subsequently won, but also suffered a big bruise on my cheek from one elbow during a tackle.

By the time the game finished, this bruise was quite noticeable and it was this that caused her to come on to me to deal with it by dabbing it with witch hazel from our medical bag.

It didn't take much coaxing to get her to move round to the back of the pavilion and she even said, after I had kissed her, thanking her for her ministrations on me, that she loved the smell of a sweaty man like I was then as we kissed, holding each other tight.

She wasn't a virgin and knew what she could feel inside my shorts could be hers and made no move to stop me from getting my hand up under her sweater to feel an unfettered breast. With me rubbing this tit, she began rubbing my now throbbing erection and I groaned that if she kept on doing that, I would make a mess of my shorts. So she stopped doing this and pulled me down onto the grass and didn't stop me from lifting up her skirt and pulling down her knickers.

I quickly got my shorts off and had the pleasure of putting myself up into my first woman for my first fuck. It was such an excitement it being my first time, that it didn't take long with me humping away to come inside that lovely hot interior of her body, not ever thinking of using a condom, but thankfully learned later that she was on the pill.

Overall, it was a hasty and hurried but enjoyable fucking of my first time in this act and it couldn't have been that bad, for she wanted me again a few days later. But this time, we were able to get well away from other people to be able to strip off and be completely naked the next time we fucked. She even went down on me afterwards though it wasn't until

I was always dressed in my military uniform and I think this helped in my wooing of her, escorting her to various restaurants until I finally got invited back to her flat. This was then the first time that we went to bed together and we both loved the sex we had and I became a frequent visitor and would often stay overnight when not on duty at the barracks.

My father was really delighted when I was promoted to captain and I was glad that this pleased him, what with me not going to university and then going into the legal profession like him. But this joy was short lived, for it was only a few weeks later that I was called into the commander's office to be told that my father had died of a sudden heart attack.

I was shell shocked for he was only fifty six years old and here I was now, a twenty four year old orphan. I was given immediate compassionate leave to be able to return home to see to the funeral etc. Nella was in tears when I turned up and glad that I was there to take care of everything. I think I was thankful on her behalf that he had collapsed while in his office in town and not at home with her having to see him dead in the house.

But she calmed down and attended the funeral by my side and I was surprised at the number of people who turned up, even having the mayor and many councillors as well as inhabitants from the village. At the wake, which was held in the village hall, for there were too many people for the house to hold, I was pulled aside by our solicitor who told me that I was now a wealthy young man, him knowing that all of the money in the bank, the house and land was now mine. This was made official a few days later at a meeting in his office.

I think it had been in the back of my mind that I only joined the army to please my father and now saw no point at putting my life at risk now in the event of our regiment being sent off to war in some foreign country and so on my return to the barracks, handed in my resignation as a captain in the Queen's army. It was accepted with regret and I finally left the army and was no longer required to wear that uniform.

I moped about my house for a week, out shooting anything that moved on our land, consoling Nella who had been left some money too, and finding out that she was willing to stay on as before in her duties. But I needed some solace myself and so spent quite a few days off and on at the flat that Mavis lived in.

I cried that first night in bed and she soothed me as only a woman can and didn't mind me just sucking on her breast like a small child. But that passed and we carried on then by having sex every night that I stayed there, but I was now at a loss as to what I should do with my future.

Then came the urge to start stealing jewellery again, but not just the odd item but making a proper killing of it for didn't I have a fence? So I started looking at jewellery shops that I might be able to rob, looking at those in towns outside of London.

It was now when Morris, the brother of Mavis turned up. Now I had known for some time that she had a brother but she had been quite vague as to where he was, but I soon found out from him after he had been back a couple of days.

He'd spent the last five years in prison for burglary which gave me much thought that he might just be agreeable to help me. He helped me in another way though I think it was for his pleasure more than mine. I'd been staying at the flat for a couple of days and was left alone with him as Mavis still had work to go to.

'Do you like fucking Mavis?' he asked me after breakfast.

'Yes,' I replied and then had him shock me.

'Would you like to fuck me too?' he asked. I was gob smacked.

'Er….I don't know what to say,' I stuttered, trying to get my mind around what he had asked.

'Just say yes. You've fucked her so why not fuck the brother. You'll like it,' he said, and I wondered if he was having me on.

'Er, er, have you done much of this then?' I asked, not really thinking of what to say...

If you enjoyed this sample then look for **Prison Sex Slave**.

Also by this Author:

The Painted Sword

Cruise Control

Wild Pleasures

Lending My Beloved

Lady of Cuckolds

Lady of Pleasure

Lady Magenta

Sexually Overdosed

Meeting My Fancy Dear

Prison Sex Slave

Chasing A Shadow

The Hostel

The Island

Thirst for Drugs and Pleasure

Forgotten Identity

Grey Memories

Chronos: Time Machine

The Hard Bomber

Honeymoon Abduction

The Yacht Sins

About the Author

Writing has always been a passion of mine. Ever since I was little I used to scribble on any blank paper I could find for any story that would come to mind, mostly tales of magic and happy endings.

Then I stopped. I blamed it all on growing up and finding out there's no such thing. For a while, I focused on my job, paying rent, and having enough to money to spoil myself.

One night I had this vivid dream of an erotic encounter that I woke up hot and panting. So I grabbed my laptop to write it down trying to relive the feeling. The pages kept on growing even though I've already written most of what I could remember. Everyday, I added something new to the story and my characters just came to life that I could see them in my head and watch their story unfold like an old movie.

And just like that, I'm hooked! Getting my mojo back, I couldn't help but share my stories to the world hoping others would enjoy it as much as I do.

Check my page on Amazon and my blog for Updates and interesting info.

Author Central - http://www.amazon.com/Amy-Redek/e/B00A48NQ72/
Author Blog - http://amy-redek.awesomeauthors.org/

If you enjoyed any of my books then please share the love and click like on my books in Amazon.

If you write me a review and send me an email I will send you a free book, or many.
(Just know that these emails are filtered by my publisher.)

Good news is always welcome.

One Last Thing, For Kindle Readers...

When you turn the page, Kindle will give you the opportunity to rate this book and share your thoughts on Facebook and Twitter. If you enjoyed my writings, would you please take a few seconds to let your friends know about it? Because... when they enjoy they will be grateful to you and so will I.

Thank You!

Amy Redek
amy_redek@awesomeauthors.org

www.ingramcontent.com/pod-product-compliance
Lightning Source LLC
Chambersburg PA
CBHW071358170626
46811CB00003B/1169